SUMMY

I so don't do
mysteries /

33387003704212

I SO DON'T DO MYSTERIES

I SO DON'T DO MYSTERIES

Barrie Summy

DELACORTE PRESS

Published by Delacorte Press
an imprint of Random House Children's Books
a division of Random House, Inc.
New York

This is a work of fiction. Names, characters, places,
and incidents either are the product of the author's imagination or are used fictitiously.
Any resemblance to actual persons, living or dead, events,
or locales is entirely coincidental.

Visit us on the Web! www.randomhouse.com

Educators and librarians, for a variety of teaching tools,
visit us at www.randomhouse.com/teachers

Library of Congress Cataloging-in-Publication Data

Summy, Barrie.
I so don't do mysteries / Barrie Summy. — 1st ed.
p. cm.
Summary: When thirteen-year-old Sherry is visited by the ghost of her mother, asking
Sherry to help solve a case involving rhinoceros poaching at the San Diego Wild Animal
Park, Sherry's involvement not only helps save the rhinos, but it also brings mother and
daughter closer together than ever before.
ISBN-13: 978-0-385-73602-2 (hardcover : alk. paper)
ISBN-13: 978-0-385-90583-1 (Gibraltar lib. bdg. : alk. paper)
ISBN-13: 978-0-385-73603-9 (pbk. : alk. paper) [1. Ghosts—Fiction. 2. Mothers and
daughters—Fiction. 3. Rhinoceroses—Fiction. 4. San Diego (Calif.)—Fiction. 5. Mystery
and detective stories.] I. Title. II. Title: I so do not do mysteries.
PZ7.S9546Ias 2008
[Fic]—dc22
2007037413

Printed in the United States of America

10 9 8 7 6 5 4 3 2 1

First Edition

In memory of my parents,
Stan and Eileen Cox,
who divided the world into
meat-and-potato and dessert books

HEARTFELT AND EVERLASTING THANKS TO

RACHEL VATER—the smartest, savviest, and most loyal agent in the whole entire universe. I'm thrilled (and still amazed) you picked me for your team.

WENDY LOGGIA—Editor Extra-Extra-Extraordinaire. Sherry and I are eternally grateful for your brilliance. And your thoroughness, enthusiasm, and humor. You so rock!

DENNY'S CHICKS—Kelly Hayes, Kathy Krevat, and Sandy Levin—the best critique group a girl could ever wish for. Seriously. I couldn't have done it without you.

MTW—a unique online group of supersupportive girly-whirly writers with pots of noodles.

OTHER TERRIFIC PEOPLE—Detective Sergeant Joe Bulkowski, who knows lots of police stuff and is willing to share; the Unfamous Nieces, especially psychic babysitter Stef; Carlene Dater, for her critiques and coffee breaks; Judy Duarte, for her guidance and great advice; and Mr. Peter Magee, my phenomenally inspirational high school English teacher.

MY SISTERS—Susan Cox and Sheilagh Scott, who are always up for a l-o-n-g phone call and who know dangerously too much about me to be left off this list.

MY FAMILY—Stan, Stephen, Drew, and Claire—for believing even when it meant more fast food and less clean laundry. And especially to Mark, who's always willing to calculate odds, drive kids, and discuss plot in the middle of the night. Thanks for putting up with me, guys.

Yikes.

I slam my hand down on the paper.

Sucking in a deep breath, I peek under my palm.

Yikes again.

A fat red F shimmers before my eyes, its wide arms swaying, mocking me, calling me lame names.

"How'd you do, Sherry?" the always-gets-an-A nerd behind me asks.

Scrunching my paper into a ball, I say, "Just peachy." Then I stand and swing my backpack over my shoulder. "I know more about genetics than I could ever use in this lifetime." Even with an F, I figure this is true.

Nerd asks, "What'd you get on the essay question?"

There was an essay question? It's so time to blow this formaldehyde stink hole. I shuffle down the aisle, the backs of my flip-flops slap-slapping my heels. As I pass the wastepaper basket, I drop my test in.

Then I give a mighty shove to the heavy metal classroom door. With a groan, it swings open onto the breezeway and fresh Phoenix air.

Thud.

"Ow!" a male voice says.

Uh-oh. That doesn't sound good.

I look behind the door.

Ack. Major tragedy. I just door-whacked Josh Morton, the coolest, cutest eighth grader at Saguaro Middle School. In Arizona. Quite possibly in the entire Southwest. I've only been nonstop crazy about Josh since September, when I spotted him in a very small Speedo at a water polo game.

Hunched over and leaning against the stucco wall, he's holding a hand against his nose and groaning.

"I'm sorry, really sorry, really," I babble. "I just flunked a test and was kind of taking out my frustration on the door."

"Yeah?" He gives me a slight smile—well, more like a big grimace. Then, with a gorgeous shoulder, he gestures toward the door. "Science?"

"Yeah." I shrug. "Like that's even useful."

"I hear you." Behind his hand, Josh sniffs.

"You okay? Can I do anything?" I can't believe I attacked Josh Morton with a door. I can't believe I, a seventh grader, am finally

2

talking to him. Nervously twirling a few strands of hair around my index finger, I add, "I feel horrible."

"I'm okay." He straightens, nodding. "I'm okay."

I take a deep breath and inhale a chlorine + soap scent. I love, love, love it. I absolutely must have some of this Eau de Josh for my locker.

"Sherry, right?" He raises dark eyebrows over deep blue eyes.

"Yup, yup, yup." I sound like the flags at the front of the school, *fwap*ping in the wind against the pole.

"I'm Josh Morton."

Believe me, I so know who you are. "Hi."

I can't come up with anything else to say, but at least I look good in my jeans and my new long-sleeved, open-neck T-shirt that perfectly matches my lavender eye shadow.

He removes his hand from his nose. Then he wrinkles it like an adorable little bunny sniffing the air for lettuce or carrots.

This is the closest I've ever stood to Josh and, therefore, the first time I notice the sprinkling of freckles across his nose. I squint. Yes, if connected carefully, they'd spell out my initials.

"Is something wrong?" He's staring at me.

"Not at all."

Last month's *Seventeen* listed twenty suggestions for memorable first meetings with a potential boyfriend. Nowhere did they mention a brutal door-whacking encounter, but it seems to be working. I'll write a letter to the editor so they can add it as method number twenty-one.

Suddenly Josh clamps a hand firmly over his nose. With his free hand, he hauls his backpack up from the sidewalk. "Gotta go." Without even a glance at me, he's off and running.

I watch his shaggy hair bounce against the collar of his black Death by Stereo T-shirt, which rides up to reveal the grooviest plaid boxers above sagging jeans. Sigh. There's something about a guy who sags.

Then I see a dotted trail of blood in Josh's wake. Oh no. I follow the spatters to the nurse's office and stop outside the entrance. My stomach sinks like the *Titanic*.

I crushed the nose of the guy I've been crushing on for six months.

In my living room later that afternoon, I'm nestled in a beanbag chair, scarfing down a Hot Pocket. It's a pretty peaceful moment, with my eight-year-old brother, Sam, gone for practice at the ball field and my dad still at work.

Then I hear the garage door open.

Seconds later, Dad strides in, shoulders back. He has a big smile on his face. "Sherry, we need to talk."

Ack. What's he doing home early? What do we need to talk about? He couldn't know about the sucky science test. No way the online grades are already posted. And he wouldn't be smiling.

Dad pops Céline Dion, his fave lame singer, in the CD player, then sits across from me in his La-Z-Boy.

Ack. Eek. "What is it?"

He doesn't answer right away, just keeps grinning wide like a frog.

"Dad! Dad! Are you okay?" Then it hits me. "You won the Powerball! You're giving me a no-limit Visa card and a Corvette with a DVD player for when I can drive in three years. And you'll finally pay for me to get highlights!"

"Sherry"—my name comes out all distorted because of his stretched-out froggy lips—"Paula and I are getting married. On Saturday."

It's like he dumped smelly swamp water over my head. And my Visa card, cool Corvette and foxy highlights.

"Saturday!" I screech. "As in the day after tomorrow? You said it would be this summer at the earliest." And I'd been counting on him coming to his senses by then.

"I know, pumpkin. But, well, there's an unbelievable Internet special for Hawaii," Dad says, "and, like you, Paula has next week off for spring break. So we decided to move things up a bit. I'll tell Sam tonight."

I bury my head in my hands.

Paula, aka The Ruler, is a math teacher at school who really lives up to her nickname. She looks like a ruler—tall and skinny with ramrod-straight posture. And she's a major control freak. I mean, she hands out detentions like candy, and don't even try taking a cell phone into her class. Not to mention her annoying habit of constantly contacting the parents of struggling students. Which is how she hooked up with my dad.

I shudder to think she'll actually be part of my family. She already has too much influence over my dad. Which means she already has too much influence over my life. Basically, The Ruler loves rules. Rules about how many minutes I should read each evening, which TV shows I can watch, how much screen time I get, how much phone time I get, who I can hang out with, when I can get a MySpace. It's frustrating and nauseating and wrong.

And now full-on stepmotherhood is only two days away.

Dad's droning on and on about wedding plans and Internet specials and Hawaii and San Diego and me.

Say what? I lift my head and tune back in to discover he wants to banish me to my great-aunt Margaret's in San Diego, while he and The Ruler hit Kauai's beaches.

I stand. "I'm not going to San Diego." I zap him with a don't-mess-with-me look. "I have plans for spring break, important plans, plans that were planned eons ago."

"Sherry—"

"You are not ruining my life. I"—and I jab my thumb into my chest—"can do that all on my own."

You know how you have a private place where you go when you just can't take the world anymore? A place where you can shove an entire Fruit Roll-Up in your mouth all at once without embarrassment? A place where you expect to be totally alone? My place is the ornamental pear tree in our backyard. My mom planted it when I was born.

So here I am, at dusk, lying on my stomach on a bumpy branch, staring down at a turtle-shaped sandbox and crying my eyes out. I can't believe Dad is getting remarried. On Saturday. To The Ruler. My life is totally ruined.

My spring break is totally ruined too. My spring-break plans have been in place for months: spend time with my girlfriends, shop at the mall, eat junk food, and sleep till noon. Very important stuff.

And even more important is my BBSRP (Brilliant But Simple Romance Plan), which goes like this: I spend time at Video World; Josh and I hook up; I wow him with my video-game skills, my conversation, my clothes, my makeup; he falls for me; he's a great kisser; we become one of those hip middle school couples everyone admires. Finally, he asks me to the Eighth Grade Graduation Dance, and I pick out the perfect dress from Sequins, an ultracool store in the mall.

Although, after this morning's door incident, the plan may need some tweaking.

Naturally, my bratty little brother gets to stay in Phoenix with Grandma Baldwin, who always says she can only handle one of us at a time. And it's never me. Like I'm trouble? Puh-leeze.

My grandmother seriously needs to learn about forgiveness. And a sprinkling of Prozac on her scrambled Egg Beaters wouldn't hurt either. So I was involved in a little incident with her darling parakeet? It happened way in the past.

When I was ten, Grandpa Baldwin had a humongous heart attack, causing him to drive off the highway and smash into a giant saguaro cactus. Grandpa, a nonbeliever when it came to a low-fat diet and seat belts, died immediately upon impact, but Grandma,

8

safely buckled, was totally unharmed. Right after the crash, a bazillion birds rose up from the surrounding cacti and thorny trees, screeching and flapping their wings. Like a big, noisy bird blanket, they covered the car. Grandma sat statue still, positive Grandpa's spirit was choosing one of the whacked-out birds as its new home. Can you say crazy? She also believes in ghosts and aura combing.

Since then, Grandma's backyard has been crammed with bird feeders and birdhouses. Also, she used to own an annoying pet parakeet named Soul. They'd chill together in the kitchen for cozy chats about the afterlife. The last time I slept over at Grandma's, Soul followed me to the bathroom, where he began pecking on the window. Anyone could see he wanted out for a little fly. Unfortunately, Soul chose to hang with the neighbor's cat, and the rest is a messy story of feathers and guts on Grandma's driveway. And, for the record, I still say it was a complete coincidence that all this took place after Grandma sent me to bed early for mouthing off.

Anyway, my BBSRP will never, ever become reality if I'm exiled to San Diego. Arms wrapped around the tree branch, I cry till I run out of tears, hiccup a little, then get mad. I sit up, cross my arms and lean against the trunk. Then I swear. Every cussword I've ever heard flies out of my mouth. Great release. I highly recommend it—except, make sure you're truly alone.

Stomping my foot on the branch, I let loose a particularly offensive string of words.

"Sherlock Holmes Baldwin!" a voice says.

I freeze. Despite the eighty-degree weather, goose bumps pop up all over my arms and legs. Slowly, slowly, I look around for the owner of that familiar voice. Nobody.

"I did not raise you to use that kind of language."

"Mom?" I squeak. I catch a faint whiff of coffee, my supercop mother's favorite beverage. This can't be happening.

"Mom?"

Silence.

"Mom?" It can't be her. Can it?

"Just a minute." The voice is impatient. "I'm having trouble landing."

This is weird. Mega weird. And mega freaky-deaky.

Because my mother? She was killed in the line of duty a year and a half ago.

chapter 3

I must be losing my mind. I start freaking out, inhaling humongous amounts of air. Palm over my pounding heart, I force myself to breathe evenly. In through the nose, out through the mouth.

The smell of coffee is suddenly stronger, like when someone's using the grinding-machine thingie at the grocery store. The branch above me dips and bounces.

"Mom?" I whip my head up. "Is it really you?"

"Yes, it is," she says, "even though you can't see me."

A Play-Doh-ish lump sticks in my throat. That voice—I never thought I'd hear it again.

We sit there, both of us sniffling. At least, I sit there. For all I know, my invisible mom's standing on her head.

I swallow hard. "I miss you."

"Me too, pumpkin." It comes out all strangled.

Tears start rolling down my cheeks. With the back of my hand, I wipe them away. I croak out a nonword.

Right at this hugely emotional moment, a cactus wren loops by, then lands by the wide date palm in the middle of our yard. It swipes at its little dark eyes with a tattered old wing. Bizarre. Is it crying along with us?

"Crazy, isn't it?" Mom says. "All those years I made fun of Grandma, and it turns out she was right."

This time I croak out a sort-of word. "Huh?"

"About ghosts existing. That's what I am."

This is majorly not sinking in for me. Like in the summer, when the sun bakes the ground so hard and dry, it can't absorb water? Well, my brain's not absorbing this big-time-strange situation.

"Can I touch you?" I ask, hushed.

There's a whoosh, and my branch jostles. The smell of coffee is right beside me. I pat the air but don't feel anything. "I wish I could see you." I pause. "Unless you're all, you know, with the bullet hole and stuff."

"We're restored to how we looked thirty minutes before our death. I just look like myself. I still need a haircut. Remember, I canceled my appointment?"

And I do remember. "Because of your migraine." I swallow. "This is way weird."

"I had choices," she says. "I could either cross over right away or go to the Academy of Spirits or choose an animal form. I chose the Academy so I could keep an eye on you and Sam."

"Wow." I'm shocked out of my shock. Mom picked us? Shut up. She was so . . . not maternal when alive. So not there for us. She practically lived at the Phoenix Police Department. And when she was home, it was all friction and "I'm very disappointed in you, Sherry."

True, I always have lousy report cards. True, I hate trying new things, so I panic and fail. True, I've had several royal screwups. Like, once when I was baking a cake, I overfilled the mold with batter and started an oven fire. Another time, I was in charge of Sam at the beach, and I totally lost him, to the point the lifeguards had to make loudspeaker announcements, then dive in for a search. Turned out my brother had wandered off to the playground. Not to mention the gazillion times I lost keys, library books, and school assignments.

Basically, my overachiever, superambitious, workaholic mother and me are polar opposites. I spent my life looking for her attention. She spent her life looking for the next promotion. And then came the drug bust that killed her.

But now? Maybe this very strange, very freaky situation is a chance for us to get it together.

"You've been watching me and Sam?" I say.

The branch sways. I can totally imagine her in her fave position, legs crossed with her top foot wiggling and jiggling.

"Only from a distance so far. I can tell you're both taller."

I'm taller? That's all she noticed? What about my increased cleavage? Seems like a fourth of a cup size would be noticeable.

Mom sighs. "Actually, the whole Academy experience has turned out to be more than I bargained for."

13

"What do you mean?"

"I'm stuck in the beginner Prevent a Crime class. Everyone else passed. It's very embarrassing, given my background in law enforcement."

"You always rocked at work stuff. What's the deal?"

"I'm having a tough time with basic ghost skills such as flying and hanging on to a location once I get there. Also, a lot of areas that were difficult for me in life are next to impossible now."

"Huh?"

"Well"—Mom pauses—"I've always had a poor sense of direction, right?"

"Definitely dismal." I nod. "I was pretty much your personal MapQuest."

"Now I can't even find point A," she says, "never mind get from A to B. The Academy is only on the other side of town. Under Dairy Queen. But it took me months to find my way here and even longer to make contact with you."

Weird, weird, weird. Next she'll be telling me she's going on a field trip to Hogwarts. "And the Academy is what, exactly?"

"An organization that trains ghosts to protect the living. To enroll, you need prior experience in a field such as law enforcement, firefighting or PI work. And to advance through the various levels, you have to conquer your weak areas. For example, I'm currently targeting my sense of direction."

I rub my forehead, thinking how a Blizzard will never be the same for me.

"Sherry?" Mom's voice goes soft and gooey and sweet, like fresh bubble gum. "I've been watching you, and it looks as though you've gotten even more fearful of challenges since I've been gone."

"Mom, I'm fine. Really." Except for the fact that I totally freeze up in tough situations. Like a Popsicle. As in frozen solid.

"I did some research at the Academy library and found an interesting loophole in their rules." She pauses. "A loophole that would allow us to work together."

"Like . . . partners?" I picture Mom's partner—well, ex-partner—Stefanie, with her cute haircut and cool blue uniform. I smile. Then I picture a bunch of bad guys with guns and scars. I frown.

"It would be completely safe," Mom says, reading my frown. "You'd just be helping me with a little mystery solving. It would build up your self-confidence."

It feels like an undigested carnitas burrito with guac and sour cream is sitting in my stomach.

"I don't do mysteries, Mom. In case you haven't noticed, I'm not Nancy Drew." I fluff my dark hair for emphasis. "Do I look like a strawberry-blond-haired teenage detective?"

"Sherry—"

"You know me," I say. "You know I'll choke."

I can make myself sweat with memories of my many mistakes. I always flunk pop quizzes; I was held back in beginner swimming five times; I'm the star of miles of videotape of school shows where I just stand there like a moron. And the lame list goes on.

"You wouldn't be operating alone. I'd be very involved."

"No, no, no." I'm shaking my head so fast, the front of my brain has probably Jell-O-jiggled all the way to the back and vice versa.

"You can do this," Mom says gently. "You've overcome challenges before."

There's a long pause where I can imagine her twirling her dark, curly hair into a ratty knot around her index finger just like I'm doing. Same hair, same habit. In fact, with my wild shoulder-length hair and large brown eyes, people often say I take after my mom. Maybe just to be nice. But still.

Finally, she sighs. "Sherry, I need to be a little more up-front. I didn't want to put this pressure on you, but—"

"What? What?" I say. "What's going on?"

"The Academy is"—Mom clears her throat—"highly competitive. This is my last chance. If I fail this assignment"—her voice cracks—"I'll have to move on."

The heavy burrito feeling is back in my stomach. My go-getter mother is failing at something? "Move on?"

"To the afterlife reserved for Academy failures."

So I'd be losing her all over again. Right after we found each other. And to a terrible fate for which I don't want details, thankyouverymuch.

"I really need your help," she says.

Like the pitiful drummer in our school band, my heart beats all erratically. My mom needs me. My überindependent, never-turns-down-a-challenge mother needs me. And not just for babysitting but for big stuff. This is mind-blowing. "What would I have to do?"

"Someone is leaving unauthorized banana treats in the rhino enclosure of an animal park."

"And?"

"They're either using the bananas to lure the rhinos to a spot where they can shoot them or planning to poison the bananas and thus the rhinos. My assignment is to find the culprit, figure out the motive and prevent any rhino deaths."

"Why doesn't the park just tell the cops?"

"According to Academy sources, the park officials don't know there's a deadly agenda. They think it's a simple case of unauthorized treats," Mom says. "And they feel they can handle that internally."

"Of course they can." I'm big-time buying into the park-people-take-care-of-the-prob scenario.

"They most definitely cannot." She pauses. "Besides, for me to get the credit for my class, we can't let anyone else solve the case."

"You have tons of experience catching criminals. Why do you even need me?"

"My basic ghost skills and sense of direction are not up to par," she says. "It'll take us both."

"How do you even know something bad's going on?"

"A ghost who knows a ghost who knows a snitch. Typical informer situation."

"Why'd they assign you this case, anyway?" I scrunch up my face. "Like, why rhinos? Why aren't you going after the scumbags who killed you?"

"The Academy's not about personal revenge," Mom says. "And I got the rhino case because"—her voice goes all proud—"I'm advanced when it comes to connecting with live animals. I was the only one who got an A plus in the Animal Mind Control class. Who knows? Maybe all that time I spent working Canine gave me a

17

special ability. Remember Nero Wolfe, my springer spaniel? That dog could sniff out—"

Oh no. She's on a roll. I swear she loved that dog more than me. "Listen, Mom—"

"You can do it, Sherry. We can do it together."

Perched on the end of a palm frond now, the wren's glaring at me with beady eyes. Creeeepy. His feathers are thin and ratty, and he's got a bunch of wrinkled pink skin pouching out. Grooooss.

This whole situation is so not me. My stomach goes all churny. "I still don't get what I'm supposed to do."

"Go to San Diego over spring break. The rhinos are at the Wild Animal Park. You can stay at Great-aunt Margaret's."

Wham. It's like the time I rode my bike into the garage door. After years of contradicting each other, now my parents decide to act as a unit? "So you and Dad are ganging up on me?" I spit out. "Just so he and The Ruler can go on their honeymoon?" I clap my hand over my mouth to stop the words. Too late.

"The math teacher?" The branch above me shakes wildly. "Oh! Oh! Oh!"

Thud.

Sand from the sandbox sprays out onto the lawn.

"Ouch."

"Mom! Mom! You okay?"

"See what I mean about having trouble staying in a location?"

Below me, a plastic shovel stands to attention, then begins digging. I guess she's decided to hang out in the sandbox.

"I figured he'd remarry," she says, "but not so soon."

"Yeah. Well. He was pretty much a basket case after you died. She's kinda been good for him." Can you say awkward?

The shovel digs faster. "Weren't the neighbors helpful? And how about Stefanie?"

"Yeah, everyone was helpful, bringing meals and stuff. And we still see Stefanie every once in a while. But you guys were so tight from being partners for a long time that I think chilling with us makes her sad."

The shovel stops and lies down.

I have a sudden vision of Dad and The Ruler kissing. I wouldn't want Mom to witness that. Actually, I wouldn't want to witness that grossness myself. "Can you get into our house?"

"I can't cross thresholds." A toy dump truck drives slowly around the sandbox, leaving wavy tire tracks in its wake. "I can only make contact outside. And only with certain people."

"Who else besides me?"

"Well . . ." The truck bumps a wall. "No one. You're the only one."

A warm, fuzzy feeling balloons inside me. I'm special. "Not Sam?"

Mom sighs. "Even in death I have to deal with sibling rivalry?"

"Not rivalry. Just an innocent question."

"Only you."

I punch the air.

"Sherry, I saw that."

"Oops." But I can't wipe the grin off my face.

"Sherry. Sherry." She sounds panicky. "I'm fading."

"Don't leave me." My insides squeeze tight at hearing my

always-in-charge, always-decisive mom half-hysterical. And when will she be back?

The truck flies onto the lawn. "I'm slipping. I can't hang on."

I look around wildly. Where is she now? A coffee-scented breeze wafts by my ear.

Her voice is little more than a whisper. "Don't tell anyone about me."

"Sure, sure. Whatever you say." My pulse races.

"This is important. It's an Academy rule."

"I get it, Mom."

And she's gone. I can tell somehow. The air is thinner or something, which I know sounds totally bogus. Plus, the smell of coffee has disappeared. And nothing is moving in the sandbox.

The wren squawks and flaps off, the spots on his wings glowing in the dusk. Finally. He was seriously scaring me.

I shudder like a twanged rubber band. Why me? Why is my life so complicated? All I want is Josh Morton. And maybe a raise in my allowance. And I wouldn't spit at a D-free report card.

I have to help her. I can't let my mother go to a horrible flunked-out ghost world. A horrible flunked-out ghost world where we won't get to see each other.

Whack. A stick hits the top of my head. "Sam!" I scream. So much for privacy in the pear tree.

My brother, his hair stick-uppier than usual, squints at me from under the tree. He raises his skinny little arm to launch another stick. "Dinner!"

"Throw that, and you'll live to regret it."

He waves a handful of twig ammo.

"Do your friends know you wet the bed last week?"

He lowers his arm.

I really should go easy on the shrimpy jerk. After all, now I have proof positive that I'm Mom's favorite. Plus, poor Sam is stuck in Phoenix for spring break with Grandma Baldwin, who farts and snores through the evening television lineup.

While I get to go to San Diego.

And save Mom's afterlife.

chapter 4

Fifteen minutes later I'm sitting at the kitchen table with a plate of rubbery whole-wheat spaghetti and ground turkey covered in runny fat-free tomato sauce. The Ruler's cooking dinner for us. Again. She's a health-food nut who seriously overseasons. I swear I'm losing precious brain cells from the herbal fumes in the room.

A sideways glance at my dad's still-full plate indicates he's as into this meal as I am.

Of the three of us, Sam manages to slurp down the most pasta, by muttering over and over, "I'm an alien from Planet Worm."

Sadly, this is normal behavior for him. He doesn't *seem* weirded out about the wedding. Then again, my brother's hard to read.

If The Ruler's aware her meal is less than popular, she isn't showing it. Instead she smiles and chats and butterfly-flutters around the kitchen, refilling our water glasses and offering us brick-heavy bread and unsalted butter. Blech. Hard to believe this cheerful, friendly woman is Ms. El Stricto at school.

So I push spaghetti around my plate, biding my time and waiting for the Hawaii/San Diego discussion to begin. I'm so ready for it. I know what I want, and I know how to get it.

A mug of steaming chamomile in her hand, The Ruler pulls out a chair next to Dad and sits down, her back straight like, well, a ruler. Does she never slouch?

Dad leans toward me, elbows on the table.

Here it comes. The hairs on my arms stand. My head fills with the music they play on TV at the opening of the Olympics. Let the games begin.

"Sherry." Dad makes eye contact. "I need to book your ticket to San Diego. The Internet special runs out tonight."

Part A of San Diego scheme: Loudly reject adult's suggestion.

"San Diego?" I screech. "What about hanging out with my friends during spring break?"

"We've been over this." Dad runs his hand through already-tousled hair.

The Ruler bites boring beige lipstick off her lips.

Part B: Suggest totally unacceptable solution.

"If I have to go somewhere, I'd rather go to Hawaii with you two." I grimace inside.

The Ruler sits up straighter. If that's possible.

"Sherry, you're old enough to know about honeymoons." Beads of sweat dot Dad's forehead.

Sam pipes up. "What do you mean?"

Dad says, "Go play video games."

"Can I play LA Mugger?" Sam asks.

"Sure, sure." Dad waves him toward the living room.

Part C: Act helpful.

"LA Mugger is rated T for 'teen,' " I mention, always the concerned, vigilant older sister. "Full of violence."

"It's okay this one time," Dad says through gritted teeth. After Sam is safely out of the kitchen, he looks at me, unblinking. "You're not coming to Hawaii. Don't even start."

Part D: Mimic hurt feelings.

I stick out my lower lip.

"Would it help," The Ruler asks, "if I checked with my sister in Scottsdale to see if Sherry could stay with her?"

Part E: Reject all solutions offered by adults.

"Stay with a total stranger?"

"Well"—the Ruler sips from her mug—"she does have a daughter about your age."

"Still a stranger," I say.

Part F: Act like you just dreamed up a new solution, then state real objective.

I snap my fingers. "I have an idea."

Relief washes over Dad's face. "What, pumpkin?"

"Why doesn't Junie come to Great-aunt Margaret's with me? My spring break wouldn't be totally destroyed, 'cause I'd still have a friend to hang with." Junie is my superbrainy, can-definitely-solve-a-mystery best friend.

"Take a friend?" Dad frowns.

"She'd have more fun in San Diego with a friend," The Ruler says. "And Junie Carter's very levelheaded."

I've known Junie for ages, ever since my first time in beginner swimming, when she passed and I didn't. We are hugely different and make great best friends because of it. I help her with social and fashion stuff. I've even offered to give her love advice, but she doesn't want it, says she doesn't have time for crushing on guys right now.

Personally, I don't understand how she turns it off. I mean, whether I want him to or not, Josh Morton barges into my brain. Anywhere. Anytime. I can be in the middle of a pre-algebra test or reading the current boring book for English or loading the dishwasher, when suddenly he'll appear and take over my entire mind. And if I happen to see him at school, well, just forget about me being able to concentrate on anything else for the next few periods.

Junie is überfocused on academics. She's all about Principal's Honor Roll and factoring and science experiments. I've never stumped her with a homework question. She's way, way smart. And it's going to take way-way smarts to save my mother. That's why Junie positively must come to San Diego with me. I know it'll be tricky getting her to solve the mystery without telling her about my mom. But I can do it.

✕ ✕ ✕

Dad calls Junie's mom and explains the situation.

There's silence on his end, which means she must be yakking away.

"Southwest Airlines," he says. "I haven't actually booked her ticket yet."

More silence. Except for the sound of Dad cracking his knuckles.

"I'll have to check with Margaret," he says, "but I don't see why three girls would be a problem."

Three? Three? My stomach drops. What three? What's going on?

"The Hawaiian Sands." He sounds puzzled.

Finally, he hangs up. "It's a go," he says, his voice all monotone.

I visualize Elmer's glue on the soles of my tennies so that I won't leap up with excitement.

Staring at me, Dad continues. "Turns out Junie's parents want to take a trip with Junie's aunt and uncle."

Oh no. I see where this is heading. The third person. Junie's cousin, Awful Amber.

"They want to send Amber to San Diego as well," he says. "She can keep an eye on you two. Plus, she has her driver's license, so you'll be less work for Margaret."

Yuck. This is horrible, dreadful, terrible. Junie won't be happy either. Awful Amber is seventeen years old, which means she's had a few extra boob-growing years. And she has definitely taken advantage of the time. And she's got fantastic emerald eyes, a creamy, zit-free complexion and straight, blond, behaves-itself hair. With all this going for her, you'd think she'd be nice. Not even close. She's mean and stupid. With Amber on the beach, Junie and I might as well be stinky seaweed. And a stupid, mean, beautiful third person will only complicate my mystery solving.

I sigh.

Dad sighs.

The Ruler's glowing like a bride-to-be. "What's the matter with you two? Junie's going with you, Sherry. And having her driving cousin along will give you more freedom." Then she shifts her gaze to Dad. "And you're getting what you want. At least, I hope you are." She lifts her narrow shoulders in confusion. "I don't see the problem."

"Oh, you will," Dad answers.

chapter 5

The next afternoon I'm leaning against the front of the giant stone saguaro cactus in the school courtyard. Like a lizard, I'm grooving on the bright sun and warm granite and the sweet smell of flowers blooming. Minding my own business. Mulling over life. I can't help but grin at last night's events. Junie's parents and her aunt and uncle got the *same* Internet special, with the *same* flight and *same* hotel, as my dad and The Ruler. Dad and The Ruler were not impressed.

Then I'm thinking about Josh Morton and hoping we meet up out here. Most students cross through the courtyard between classes. Next my thoughts drift to *The Ear, the Eye and the Arm*, which I never finished reading for English. Then I'm back to Josh and majorly daydreaming about him. He's walking in front of me with yellow DC shoes and low-riding Dickies jeans. Wow, but he looks gorgy great. I cannot get enough of his chlorine-bleached hair. He turns, opens his amazing mouth and says—

"Sherry!"

I blink in surprise.

"Sherry!" Brianna yells as she runs toward me.

End of *fantástico* daydream. Enter my friend Brianna, cute-ish, dumbish, boy crazy.

Junie trails behind Brianna, her backpack swinging over her shoulder, her face shiny.

Brianna tucks an auburn-streaked strand of hair behind her ear. "Big, big news. Just let Junie catch up, and we'll fill you in."

Junie arrives, panting.

That girl has got to get some serious exercise. Me too. Especially before I parade around on a beach dressed only in a skimpy bikini, with Amber as competition. "What's up?"

"You tell her, Brianna. You were there." Junie wipes sweat off her forehead.

"It happened like this." Brianna juts out a hip and grasps it. "Margo told Sara who told me that during third period Josh Morton asked Kristen if you liked video games."

My insides turn to mush. Josh Morton's asking questions about me. Even after the door fiasco. Yowser.

"Sherry." Junie shakes my shoulder. "Earth to Sherry."

I feel a goofy grin stretching across my face. "I'm here." My voice sounds dreamy. "So? What did Kristen say?"

" 'I don't know,' " Brianna answers.

"What? You didn't find out?"

"Kristen said, 'I don't know.'" Junie pushes her glasses up her nose.

"Oh." I twirl my hair. "Well, send it through the grapevine that I totally kill at video games."

"I already did. But the big question is . . ." Brianna pauses for dramatic effect. "Will you let him win?"

I consider the idea for about half a sec, then shake my head. "No."

"I knew it," Junie says.

Suddenly Brianna punches my upper arm. "Josh is coming this way."

"Say what?" I clench my teeth.

Brianna eyebrow-telegraphs *Behind you and to the left.* "It's Josh."

I finger-comb my hair. To no avail, I'm sure. Help.

"Twenty feet." Brianna flaps her hands all hyper, like we're having the most exciting conversation the cactus statue has ever heard.

My heart's trying to jump out of my chest.

"Ten feet." Brianna laughs inanely.

This girl better never consider acting; she'd starve. I feel a twitch over my right eye.

"Five feet." Brianna's voice drops to a whisper.

I'm going to explode with anticipation. Acting cool is out of reach.

"Four, three, two, one. We have contact." Brianna's jaw hangs open. "Contact missed." Her head swivels. "Negative one, negative two, negative three—"

"Stop," I say, flushing the color of Junie's face after PE class.

Josh Morton totally blew me off. In front of everyone. I'm such a loser.

I blink back tears as he saunters over to a group of eighth graders. A girl with glittered-out hair sashays to him and drapes an arm around his waist.

"Maybe you better let him win at video games," Brianna says. "I'm outta here. Social studies."

My shoulders slump until I'm curved like a comma. "Get me to English," I choke out to Junie. Good thing it's the last class of the day and we sit next to each other.

Junie takes my hand. We begin what feels like a ten-mile trek to English.

My feet drag, heavy like The Ruler's homemade bread. And it suddenly occurs to me that I can't do this. How am I supposed to pull off an animated debate about a book I never finished while my spirits are lower than the grade on my last essay? I explain my position to Junie.

She stops, tilts her head to one side and chews on her tongue, thinking. "I've got the solution," she says. "Female problems."

"Yes." I'd make a victory fist in the air, but I'm too weak with depression.

She marches along, hauling me with her. "Mr. Franklin will buy it."

Our English teacher freaky-deaks at the mention of female problems. Just look like you're going to say "period" and he'll shoo you down to the nurse ASAP. And technically I am having female problems.

Female problems of the heart.

chapter

6

Carefully placing one foot in front of the other, I plod to the nurse's office. When I get there, I drop the peach-colored pass in the mesh basket on the counter and hunch over in a plastic chair, mouth-breathing because of the gross rubbing-alcohol smell. I'm the only student around.

The nurse strides over from her computer and plucks up my pass. "Sherlock Baldwin, what seems to be the problem?"

"Um, um." I'm such a bad liar.

"Cramps?"

"Um, sure."

"Let me go check your file to see if your parents okayed any **over-the-**counter meds." And she disappears into the back room.

I close my eyes. Will Midol cure a broken heart? Doubtful. But that thought opens up a whole new future career path. I'll be a scientist who invents a pill that turns heartache into a brief bout of gas. You fart, and you're immediately better, immediately over being dumped. I imagine myself accepting the Nobel Peace Prize in front of hordes of adoring fans. "It all started in the nurse's office one sunny middle school day after I was cruelly rejected by Josh Morton. Who, I might add, has amounted to nothing in life. He lives in the woods, all dirty and smelly, and only comes out to beg for money. I'll never forget what he did to me—"

"Sherry?"

Josh? I open my eyes. Ack. Eek. Awk.

"What are you here for?" He stands in the doorway, a file folder under his arm.

"Um, um, um," I sputter.

"You okay?"

Do I see worry wrinkle his forehead?

I force the words out. "Nothing"—I swallow—"contagious."

Scrounging-around sounds come from the back room. Please, please, please, Nurse, be a disorganized mess like me. If her file cabinet looks anything like my backpack, she won't find my paperwork until I'm in high school.

I force out more words. "How's your nose?"

"Totally fine," he says. "The door didn't even hit me that hard. My nose just bleeds easily."

I risk a joke. "So you won't be suing?"

He shakes his head, laughing. "Nah."

I've never heard him laugh before. It's deeper than I expected, and I am digging it.

"Let me drop this off with the attendance clerk." Josh waves the folder. "I'll be right back."

"Okay." Wow. Stomach jittery, hands sweaty, I hook my hair behind my ears and smooth out my T-shirt.

Josh returns and slides into a chair across from me. "I hear you're into video games," he says.

Did I mention how his Lake Havasu–blue eyes look electric when he gets excited? I can't stop staring at them. It's like I'm being sucked in.

"There's this boy-girl tournament Video World's holding over spring break," he says. "I thought we maybe could join as a team."

I start floating out of my chair with happiness. Then reality slaps me back down hard and fast. "I can't." My voice comes out flat. "I'm going out of town. My dad's getting remarried, and I'm being shipped off."

"Bummer." He sounds truly disappointed.

"To San Diego."

"Hey, I'm from San Diego. We go back a lot to visit family."

Oooooh. We're like soul mates! "How'd you end up in Phoenix?"

"My dad got transferred." Josh bends down to tie his shoe. "Worked good for me. I was kinda in with a rough crowd at school there." He straightens up and stretches out his legs.

"Oh." A tingle shimmies up my back. I'm crushing on a bad boy—well, a reformed bad boy. *Oooooh*.

"Although I did lose a year. I should be a freshman."

34

A reformed almost-a-freshman bad boy? *Oooooh!*

"Need ideas for things to do in San Diego?" Josh asks.

"Sure." I relax and lean back. Look at me. So cool, so *Cosmo,* so casually chatting with a cutie-pie guy, like I do it every day.

He squints, thinking. "The beaches, SeaWorld, Old Town, which has a haunted house." He pauses, then slaps the side of his head with his hand. "The Wild Animal Park."

The hairs on my neck poke up. Literally. First my mother brings up the Park, then Josh does. Not that I believe in any of Grandma's hocus-pocus, but, seriously, this must be a sign.

I ask, "What's so great about the Wild Animal Park?"

"Well, it's, like, this gigantic zoo, but with tons of wide-open spaces. What's really cool is that a rhino born at the Park is getting ready to give birth." Josh is talking with his hands, getting all adorably animated. "It's that whole two-generations-born-in-captivity thing. And the entire city is into it." He pulls his phone from his pocket. "Give me your number."

"I don't have a cell." I sigh. "But you can have my home number." Which I reel off.

When he's finished programming it in, he snatches up a pen and a flyer advertising a health fair. He scribbles on the back of the paper, then hands it to me. "My cell."

I glance at his number, memorize it, then slide the paper into my backpack.

Suddenly I hear the *squish-squish* of the nurse's shoes. Vaulting out of my chair, I scoop my backpack off the floor and swing it on, all in one smooth move. "Tell the nurse something came up and I had to take off, will you?"

His baby blues are wide open with surprise.

And, without even considering the consequences, I wink.

Then I'm off down the hall, out past the special-ed bus in the circular drive and hoofing it toward home. With only one teeny, but überly important, stop on the way.

chapter 7

After my errand, I hang out in my room, eat a non-Ruler dinner and kinda do some homework.

Finally it's midnight. I slowly slide open the back door, a cold latte clutched to my chest. I'm wrapped in the scratchy crocheted afghan Mom used to cover herself with to watch the news. It smells of the vanilla-bean after-shower spray she loved. My throat tightens.

As I step off the patio, the motion light flashes on. I blink in the sudden brightness at my pear tree, lit up against an inky background. Cocooned in the afghan, I take baby steps, the dewy grass licking my bare feet.

All evening, while I was stuck babysitting Sam, thoughts of me, my mom and some scary, bizarro mystery in San Diego chased each other round and round in my head. I'm having severe doubts about my sanity. I'm having severe doubts about this whole situation. If it's for real, I am so not the person for this big-time challenge. Given my history of failures.

All I want is to hang out with my mom. Really hang out with her. Like we didn't do when she was alive.

There's a lot about her I don't know. Like, what was her fave candy when she was a kid? Did she and her mom get along? How much does she miss me?

And I want my mom to know me better too. How sometimes I forget she's gone, and I go to tell her something; then, like a slap in the face, it hits me that she's not around. How bad I feel for all the mean things I ever said. How thinking about The Ruler gives me a stomachache because, although she isn't my mom, she'll get to do loads of mom things, like taking pictures of me all dressed up for prom.

The problem is, for me and my mom to spend time together, she has to stay in the Academy. Which means she has to do the mystery thing. Which means I have to do the mystery thing. Which brings me right back to the beginning. All I want is to hang out with my mom.

I toss the afghan up onto my sitting branch, then—on tiptoe— carefully place the coffee cup in a hollow in the trunk. Once I've climbed up and am mummy-wrapped in the afghan, I free one arm, retrieve the cup and pry off the lid.

Coffee—my mother's beverage of choice. Colombian, Jamaican, Food City, medium-bodied, bold, espresso: She loved them all. She downed so much coffee, she was permanently wired. Some days, I never saw her eat real food, only drink cup after cup of coffee.

On the way home from school today, I stopped at the Donut Hole. I kept the latte hidden at the back of my closet until now. My dad knows I'm not into coffee, and I didn't want to deal with his questions.

I just hope it works, and cold java summons her. I stretch out my arm, waving the cup back and forth in front of myself.

Holding my breath, I wait for some sort of sign.

Nada. Nothing.

I balance the cup in the hollow above my head, leaving the lid off, then sit, my spine curled into the trunk. Eyes squeezed shut, I conjure up an image of Mom from our last shopping trip together.

We were sitting on a mall bench outside Pat and Oscar's Restaurant, waiting for Dad and Sam. We were having a quick family dinner before Mom headed to work for third watch. Between my knees sat an overflowing Old Navy shopping bag. Mom plopped a Body Shop bag on top of my stuff, then leaned forward, closing her eyes. With circular movements, she massaged her temples.

"I can't seem to kick this headache," she said.

I chomped on a pretzel sample. "Call in to work sick."

"Can't. There's a big drug bust going down. I've got to be there."

A chunk of salt slipped down the wrong pipe, and I coughed loudly.

Mom grimaced. "Maybe I'm developing migraines." She lifted

her head, eyes still closed. "I'll eat something before taking more Excedrin."

I dug through my Old Navy merchandise, examining my new clothes, only half listening. I was more interested in figuring out what to wear to school the next day than in worrying about my mother.

And that was the night she got killed.

chapter

8

A thump rattles the trunk and tips the coffee over and down my neck. Yuck.

"How did you find me?" Mom asks, her voice pitching up with surprise. "I was in the middle of a practice flying session with my study group, when suddenly I was whooshing through the air, and *whomp!* I landed here."

I hold up the empty cup in the direction of her voice. "The Donut Hole called your name."

"Brilliant, Sherry."

Brilliant. My mother called me brilliant. I straighten my shoulders.

"I smell coffee mixed with the melon scent of your shampoo."

"Sassy Girl," I say.

"That's it." Mom switches to Intense Mode. "Did your dad get your ticket to San Diego?"

"He did." I pull up the neck of my T-shirt to mop off my skin. "For Sunday afternoon."

"Good."

"Junie and Amber are coming too."

"Remember, you can't tell them about me. And make sure Junie keeps a lid on Amber. She's too wild for you two. On the plus side, Amber has her license. She can drive you to the Wild Animal Park. That'll lessen the burden on Margaret."

I roll my eyes. She's as bossy dead as she was alive.

"I am really feeling good about this case. Everything's falling into place." Mom's branch shakes, and the leaves flutter all crazy.

Is my mother so pumped, she's doing a little dance?

"We're going to impress my instructors by preventing the rhino killings. I'll get to stay in the Academy," she says. "And you, young lady, will conquer your fear of challenges."

Her bubbly enthusiasm is contagious. Maybe she's right, and this will all work out. Come to think of it, I've definitely gotten more independent since her death. Like doing laundry, setting my alarm clock to get up for school, babysitting Sam more.

"You would not believe how excited the Academy is about us. It's been over two centuries since they've had a mother-daughter duo."

So, I'm a celebrity, spiritually speaking.

"They're allowing my study group to help us. There are four of us: me; Marie, a former cop from Oklahoma City; Alan, a former

42

FBI agent; Ray, a former federal judge. We all started the Academy together, and we've gotten really close. Marie, Alan and Ray were recently promoted to the next level. They're trying to bring me up to speed. They are so talented and so supportive." Mom's words race out at about a million miles a minute. "Sherry— you, me, them, we'll make a great team."

"Team"? Did my mother just say "team"? As in T-E-A-M? "Team" is my new fave word. Mom has never, ever asked me to be on her team before.

She goes all serious. "And you haven't told anyone about me?"

"No."

"Good going."

"Brilliant." "Team." "Good going." Wow. I'm psyched. I'm stoked. I'm jazzed. I am so going to San Diego to solve a mystery and save my mother's life—well, afterlife. Brimming over with enthusiasm, I'm waving my arms, punching the air. Then I'm kicking the air. Then I'm falling through the air, arms and legs flailing.

Thud.

Man oh man. Hard sandbox. And falling on it is becoming a mother-daughter tradition.

"Are you okay?" Mom's voice is a soft breeze by my ear.

"Yeah." I stand. "Mom, this is like a do-over for us, isn't it?"

Very gently, my hair lifts off my forehead. "That's exactly what it is, Sherry. And not many deceased mothers and living daughters get this opportunity."

I blink back tears. "I'm glad we have it."

"Me too, pumpkin."

The back door opens. Dad steps out onto the porch.

"I'm meeting with the snitch tomorrow night to see if he has any new info," Mom says. "Let's touch base again before you leave."

"Okay."

"They're having the wedding in the backyard?" She's above me now, and whispering.

"How'd you know?" I ask her.

"Sherry? Is that you out here?" Dad calls. "You all right?"

"I'm fine!" I shout. "Just give me a sec."

"I noticed gazebo arches leaning against the side wall." Mom's voice is faint. "Tomorrow's the big day, then? In the afternoon?"

Dad starts walking toward me, and the motion beam floods the yard.

I answer, "Yeah."

"I'll try . . ."

I strain to hear.

". . . to attend."

"No, no, no," I say, "bad idea. Bad idea."

But she's already gone.

chapter 9

It's just a wedding. *It's just a wedding,* I chant over and over in my head.

I can make it through this afternoon. I will be cool. I will be mature. I will not have a meltdown. Then tomorrow I'll fly to San Diego and save the rhinos for my mother so that she'll get to stay in the Academy of Spirits and hang out with me, her wonderfully amazing daughter and favorite child.

It's just a wedding. It's just a wedding.

I pull at the collar of my dress and scratch. What kind of a bride chooses ugly, striped dresses for her bridesmaids? Honestly, I look like Bert and Ernie's dorky big sister.

I sneak a sideways glance at the bridesmaid standing next to me. Ms. Gonzalez, my PE teacher. How weird is all this? First time

I've seen her out of stretchy shorts and a baggy Arizona State T-shirt. She doesn't look too great all spiffed up, especially with thick streaks of peach across her cheeks and mouth. Has the woman never heard of blending?

My own makeup is adorable, if I do say so myself. I went in for the glitter look in a big way. So, while the dress is pitiful, I'm a very sparkly bridesmaid.

My makeup is the most sophisticated aspect of this wedding. Tacky Wedding was thrown together quickly with a lot of help from Party Rentals. In our backyard, rows of metal fold-up chairs sit in front of a cheesy arch covered with plastic roses. A rectangular table close to the kitchen door holds platters of raw veggies and rolled cold cuts from Costco, and Grandma Baldwin's home-baked "lifetime harmony" wedding cake.

It's just a wedding. It's just a wedding.

I'm constantly scanning the yard and sniffing, jumpy-jittery nervous that Mom'll make an uninvited guest appearance. Knowing she can't get into our house, I tried to talk Dad and The Ruler into a romantic living-room wedding. But no go. The Ruler wanted outdoors.

Weirdly, outdoors is the only thing The Ruler insisted on. She didn't want huge, flashy, pricey. Which is what I'll insist on. Maybe she was thinking of my dad and how he's already done the big, first wedding thing. Maybe she was thinking of my mom and how her death wasn't that long ago. Who knows with The Ruler?

It's 1412 military time. The palm fronds aren't shaking. Nothing is moving in the sandbox. The ornamental-pear branches are still.

The area is secure. I'm not even sure what I'll do if Mom does show, but I'm on the lookout.

Grandma Baldwin's been busy setting up the food and plates and stuff. Now, tucking her peasant blouse into her skirt, she's finally lowering herself into a chair in the front row. She takes a Kleenex out of her burlap bag and dabs at her eyes. She mouths, "You okay?"

I nod, the chant getting louder. *It's just a wedding. It's just a wedding.*

Grandma peers over at Sam, where he's standing with my uncle, the best man. I see her wink at my brother and place her index fingers at the corners of her lips, pushing them up into a smile.

I crane my head to look at Sam. He's crying quietly while my uncle squeezes his shoulder.

It's just a wedding. It's just a wedding. The chant roars in my head.

Scan, scan, scan. Sniff, sniff, sniff. Oh no. I smell coffee. I morph into dog-at-the-park mode. Body rigid, my head moves up, down, right, left. Nose twitching, I sniff some more.

Mrs. Lucas, our next-door neighbor, is taking a seat in a chair on the lawn. Next to Junie, who gives me a little wave. Mrs. Lucas places something under her chair.

I squint. Yikety yikes. It's a cardboard cup from Starbucks.

I dash across the yard, snatch up the cup and charge into the kitchen. I quickly dump the coffee down the sink drain.

Grandma follows right on my heels. "What are you doing, Sherry?"

"Coffee." I'm panting. My mind's blank. I can't think of a single explanation for why I'd get rid of Mrs. Lucas's coffee.

47

Grandma looks at the empty cup and at the last of the tan liquid swirling down the drain. Her face softens, and she starts rubbing my back. "I understand, dear. I tear up whenever I smell coffee." She rubs under her nose. "Reminds me of your mother."

Wow.

"You should've seen me boohooing in here when I set up the percolator."

Sure enough, now that she's mentioned it, I hear a telltale *burp-burp*ing. There it is on the counter next to the toaster—a big aluminum forty-cup transmitter to the next world. Forty potential cups of Mom-calling java that wedding guests can carry around the backyard.

I yank on the cord, then slide the urn across the tile counter until it reaches the lip of the sink. Ouch. Can you say hot?

"Sherry. Stop. Right. Now," Grandma orders.

"I. Can't." I pop up the lever that opens the spigot, and as the coffee spills into the sink, tears spill down my cheeks. I can't let Mom show up in the middle of all this wedding hoopla. I can't.

"Young lady—" Grandma grips my shoulders and turns me to face her. One look at me, and her tone changes. "Oh, honey. I had no idea you were this upset." She wraps her arms around me.

I sob. So much for the cool-mature-no-meltdown thing. And think of how I'm ruining my makeup.

Grandma follows me to the bathroom. She waits quietly while I fix my mascara and eye shadow, then presses a smooth stone into the palm of my hand. "A crystal. Hang on to this. It'll get you through the afternoon. Balances you. In fact, take it to San Diego to keep you safe. I'm uneasy about that trip."

The clear stone fits easily in my palm. I run my thumb along the surface. It's a teardrop shape with a sharp point. Sharp enough to be a weapon, which is weird since my grandmother is Mrs. Spread-the-Peace. "Thanks, Grandma."

She pulls me against her narrow chest, enveloping me in some health-food store's rosemaryish brand of perfume. "Let's go, girl. You can do this."

Hand in hand, we head to the backyard, out into the blazing Arizona sun. With a wide grin at us, my dad pushes the button on our iPod, cueing the bride's entrance music.

chapter 10

The ceremony pretty much goes by in a blur.

I close my eyes and rub my index finger over the crystal at the "you may kiss the bride" part, and let the chant take over in my head at the "I now present Mr. and Mrs. Robert Baldwin" part.

On to the reception. I can handle that. It's like the last leg in a relay race. So I lost it earlier in the kitchen? Now I'm coming in for the gold.

Grandma's over at the buffet table, setting up a punch bowl of lemonade.

Lips frozen in a fake-o smile, I eyeball the backyard for signs of my mother. Still nada.

Junie wanders over to me. "What's with your neck? And your chin?"

I reach up and feel trillions of tiny bumps. Itchy bumps. My shoulders are itchy too. And my chest. I'm turning into one big hive.

"I wonder if you're allergic to something in the dress," Junie says.

"I'm definitely allergic to its ugliness," I say. "Come with me while I change."

"Pictures," my dad calls out. "Bridal party over by the ornamental pear tree."

Pictures. Yikes. Like I want to be caught on celluloid all rashed out like this.

"Keep your chin down," Junie advises.

"Stay with me," I plead. "Let me know if the rash is showing." We head over to the tree and try to find a spot where I can hide in the shadows.

"Daughter of the groom?" the photographer asks.

Where did we find him? He looks like an army general. Very GI Joe, with a buzz and incredibly straight posture. He must be related to The Ruler.

"Yes," I mumble, chin pointing south.

He stretches out an arm, no bend at the elbow. "Roy March. The bride's cousin."

I knew it. I shake his hand.

"Stand over there." He points to a very sunny spot, a spot sure to highlight my bumpy skin. Terrific.

The rest of the wedding party shows up. The Ruler jokes and laughs and beams. Even my dad is swept up in her festive mood. Sam too, who looks like a mini Dad in his tux. The photographer snaps an impromptu father-son shot where Dad and Sam are high-fiving.

Next, GI Joe lines us up, touching our shoulders and positioning our heads. He struts back to his camera and barks orders at us from behind the viewfinder.

Junie stands behind him and directs me with hand gestures, helping me find poses to hide my ravaged neck and chin.

The photographer yells for, like, the millionth time, "Sherry, look up! Eyes off your shoes."

Junie shakes her head, index finger pointing to the ground.

I bob my head up marginally, then back down.

Dad gives an exasperated "For Pete's sake, Sherry, can't you follow simple directions?"

Even The Ruler is no longer bubbling like champagne.

GI Joe strides over, grasps my chin in one hand and my forehead in the other and angles them up. He frowns at my skin. "I'll have to do touch-ups."

I snap.

"No more pictures!" I scream over my shoulder as I fly into the house and lock myself in the upstairs bathroom. Forget about not losing control. At least I manage to hold back the tears until after the door lock clicks into place.

What has happened to me? I've turned into a geyser with all this crying. I'm probably dehydrated.

I slurp some water from a paper cup, ignoring the science info printed on the side. Thanks to The Ruler, even brushing our teeth is an educational experience. Then I peel off the ugly bridesmaid dress and stuff it in the wicker trash basket.

Standing back from the mirror over the sink, I gaze at all the angry red bumps. From the waist up, I look like a lizard alien from Planet Grotesque. The rash is getting worse. It's up to the circles under my eyes.

Knock, knock.

I don't answer. Lizard aliens from Planet Grotesque don't talk. They do listen, though, and I press my ear to the door. It's Junie and The Ruler.

"Maybe it'd be better if you talked to her," The Ruler says. She actually sounds concerned.

"Okay," Junie says.

"Let her know she's not needed for any more pictures."

Like that was going to happen, anyway.

The Ruler adds, "Her uncle's picking up some topical cream and Benadryl from the pharmacy."

There's silence for a moment. I guess Junie's waiting for The Ruler to leave. Junie's a great friend, the perfect friend. I couldn't have picked a better best friend.

Knock, knock.

"It's me," Junie says.

"Can you grab me some clothes?" I unlock and crack the door.

Within minutes, she's in the bathroom, shorts and a T-shirt draped over her arm. Her eyes widen. "You're a mess."

"Tell me about it." I slip on my outfit, then drop the lid on the toilet seat and sink down. "Everything about my life is a mess, a big, ginormous, awful disaster."

Junie puts a hand on my shoulder.

And I think maybe it's her hand, that physical connection with my best friend, that tips me over the edge. Junie, the one person who can help me out of the overwhelming craziness and scariness of ghost mother + mystery challenge + wedding + rash + Josh.

Whatever the exact reason, it's like I can't help myself. Before I realize it, my mouth is open. And the words are tumbling out, pushing and elbowing each other in their rush to exit. I blurt out the whole entire story of my mother and the rhino mystery at the Wild Animal Park.

Junie's jaw drops. "Your mother's a ghost?"

I nod.

She crosses her arms. "And you have to help her solve a mystery?"

I nod again. "This is the biggest, most important challenge of my life. I can't do it without you. You have to help me."

"Oh, Sherry." Junie's face is long with concern. "Oh, Sherry." She shakes her head. "Oh, Sherry."

chapter 11

All the guests have left. I'm sitting on the landing at the top of the stairs, listening to the normal sounds below. Sam's playing Wii Sports, probably now changed into his fave Diamondback T-shirt. Dad and The Ruler are in the kitchen, their voices so faint I can't decipher what they're saying.

I'm not feeling so normal inside. I'm feeling queasy, like I rode the jerky, spinning Scrambler ride one too many times. I just broke a huge Academy rule. And what if Junie doesn't believe me? Now what's going to happen to me and my mother?

Suddenly I can hear voices. It's Dad and The Ruler, standing at the bottom of the staircase.

"I'll check on her," The Ruler says.

No, no, no. Leave me alone, evil straight-spined woman.

"Are you sure, Paula?" my dad asks. "You know how prickly she can be."

Moi? Prickly?

"I'm sure." The bottom stair creaks. "I want to see how her rash is doing."

Yeah, yeah. She wants to laugh at my freakish skin. Unlike my naive dad, I'm not taken in by her phony-baloney niceness act.

"And I haven't given her the bridesmaid gift yet," she says.

A gift? *Oooooh.* Things are looking up. I scoot back to my room, hop on the bed and open my book.

At my door, The Ruler smiles. "It's upside down."

I scowl and drop the book on the carpet.

She looks around, nodding. It's the first time she's been in here and, therefore, the first time she's been exposed to its dazzling decor. "Very innovative."

I can't help but agree. At Home Depot, I whipped up a special batch of paint for the walls and created a gorgeous, rich color I call "turquoise + sea green." Then I tossed in a few handfuls of glitter. The stunning result is shimmering, sparkling walls. Miracle of all miracles, I found the perfect bedspread, with waves of blues and greens, onto which I sewed different-shaped sequins. Next I glued colored glass that looks like gemstones around the door frame and across the windowsills. It's like living in a pirate's treasure chest.

Sadly, though, I've been unable to locate turquoise + sea-green gravel for my aquarium. I am hugely into my fish, all named after fairy-tale characters, and always coordinate their space with mine. We're happiest when our environments match and mesh.

The Ruler sets a wrapped box on the dresser and walks toward me with a tube of ointment. "Let's take a peek."

I tip my head back so that she can see my neck where the rash is the worst. Her fingers feel cool on my hot skin. This is the most relaxed I've felt all day. Weird.

"Good. It's going down." The Ruler hands me the ointment. "This is stronger than the one I brought up before. Don't use it on your face."

"How will I look tomorrow?"

"Good enough to get on a plane."

I let out a sigh of relief.

"Have you ever had this kind of reaction to stress before?"

"Stress? No, no, no. I'm allergic to the bridesmaid dress."

"I don't think it was the dress," she says.

Well, I am überly stressed. What with my mom, the Academy, the wedding. I mean, who wouldn't be stressed to the max?

The Ruler goes into the bathroom.

Yikes. I hope she doesn't spot my bridesmaid dress in the trash.

She returns with a science Dixie cup and a pink pill. No mention of the dress. She gives me the cup and pill. "More Benadryl."

While I'm swallowing the pill, she says, "I think it's time you started calling me Paula." With a small grin, she adds, "Of course, you can still refer to me as The Ruler at school."

She walks to the dresser for the gift. "Let's trade."

"You're not getting much of a deal," I say, crumpling the cup as I hand it to her.

"Oh, I think I am."

I sense there's a hidden message in her words but am not getting sucked into an "I'm looking forward to being your stepmother" conversation. I don't need a stepmother. I have a mother. A real one. Well, a real, dead one.

chapter 12

I bound out of bed way early the next morning. Our flight isn't until two, but I gotta get hold of my mother.

First thing I do is grab my brand-new cell phone off my night-stand. The Ruler, Paula, definitely knows how to choose a gift. I've wanted a cell forever. And this one is teeny and tiny and cute and shiny with perfect little buttons and a few video games.

Second thing I do is elbow on the bathroom light. I scream. The Ruler, Paula, whoever, was so wrong. I don't look cured enough to get on a plane. I look like I need to be abandoned on a desert is-land, where I can't freak out small children and pets.

I grab a half-dried-up concealer stick. The whole time I'm col-oring my face and neck, I'm thinking Mom thoughts. Scary Mom thoughts. Like, what's she going to say when she finds out I broke a major Academy rule by blabbing to Junie? Color. Worry. Color. Worry.

All of a sudden, a brilliant idea zaps me like static shock. I won't tell Mom that I told Junie. I'm sure the Academy will never figure it out, because, with all their important ghostly responsibilities, how much are they gonna stay on top of one lousy ghost, one little mystery and me?

One final swipe with the stick, and I'm ready to contact my mother. Hopefully her special snitch gave her beaucoup details, like the suspect's name, photo, address, driver's license, motive. And how about info like exactly when he plans to carry out his deadly deed?

In the kitchen, I haul down the can of French roast and the coffeemaker from the cupboard. I set them side by side on the counter. Now what?

A toilet flushes upstairs. Hurry. Hurry. Think. Think. I peel the lid off the can. Coffee smell wafts throughout the room, and a lump as big as a Ping-Pong ball jams my throat. I shake my head. No time for this. I partially fill the carafe with water, then dump in some grounds, which float around like dead ants in a swimming pool. Gross. Why do people drink this stuff?

"Whatcha doin'?"

I shriek, jump, drop the carafe. In that order. Amazingly, the carafe doesn't break but spits water + grounds all over the tile. "Look what you did," I say to Sam. "Get cleaning."

"Okay." Rubbing his eyes, he unrolls some paper towels.

My brother must be sleepwalking; he never follows my orders.

"Fine," I say. "Give me some too."

He tears off a bunch of sheets and hands them to me.

I start mopping up puddles.

"It smells like Mom in here." His voice cracks.

I look over at him, with his sleep-messy eyebrows and drooping SpongeBob pajamas. "Uh-huh."

He blinks, and a couple of tears roll down his cheeks. With a sob, he lunges at me and hangs on, like some kind of four-foot-tall munchkin-parasite.

I rub his back. "Things'll get better." Especially if I help Mom so she gets to stay in the Academy. Maybe she'll learn to contact Sam too. Mom can watch his Little League games. And if she learns to cross thresholds, she can come to our school stuff, like plays and citizen-of-the-month assemblies. We can hang together, tell her about our day, joke around, talk about what's bugging us. It could be great.

Sam gives a big, wet, mucusy sniff, then untangles himself. "You wanna drink coffee to help you remember Mom better?"

"Something like that."

He pulls a package of filters out of the lazy Susan and pinches one off. Then he expertly taps the filter gently into place, spoons in some French roast, rinses out the carafe, refills it and pours the water into the machine. After pushing the On button, he says, "I made enough for me too. Not to drink. Just to smell."

Standing next to each other, close but not touching, the two of us silently watch the coffee drip down. When it's done, I pour two mugs.

"*Scooby Doo*'s on." Sam cradles the mug between his hands and shuffles like an old man into the living room.

I wait till he's on the couch and zoned out in front of the TV, then shove open the sliding door. If I don't hurry, I'll find myself trying to explain to Dad and The Ruler why I'm up a tree with a cup of coffee.

Once outside, I follow my routine from before. Hey, why mess with success? So I get comfortable on my branch, wave the mug around over my head, then set it above me in a hollow in the trunk and think about my mom.

Within seconds, there's a humongous thud, probably measurable on the Richter scale.

"Landing, landing," my mother says.

Squawk. Squawk. Squawk.

I look up. It's the same beady-eyed wren I've been seeing around our yard. He's hugging the trunk with his wings.

"I've got to work on that." Mom says from the branch right above me. "Looks like my rough landing scared your grandfather."

"Huh?" It's like my brain suddenly empties of live thoughts.

"The wren. It's Grandpa Baldwin." She pauses. "You hadn't figured it out?"

"No one figures that kind of stuff out." I shake my head. "Why's Grandpa a bird?"

"He chose the animal option. Your grandparents, as you know, have always been bird lovers. Which is why he went with a wren form."

"Way weird." My life is veering deeper into insanity country. What happened to normal stuff like dying and getting buried in the ground? And staying there?

Mom's branch creaks. "Grandpa spends most of his time in Grandma's backyard. He likes to be near her. Plus, she keeps the bird feeder full."

I have many memories of Grandpa. He loved to wear hugely nerdy leather shorts and polka-dot suspenders, then belt out embarrassing German songs into a bratwurst/microphone. He often had a parrot on his shoulder. And he was always tossing back a handful of sunflower seeds. And never sharing, I might add. Well, except with my brother, who takes accordion lessons.

"Grandpa has offered to help us in San Diego," Mom says. "If he can fly that distance. You know, given his age."

I groan. I don't need an ancient wren that, in human form, never really liked me and now specializes in shooting me the evil eye. Besides, we've already got Junie and my mom's study group.

"He's pretty smart for an old bird, and we need all the help we can get."

"Fine. Any new scoop from the snitch? Like the names and addresses of suspects?"

"Police work isn't usually that straightforward. But he did learn that the poacher is experienced. And even though the snitch hasn't given us much, we have my study group. They are truly brilliant."

Mom clears her throat. I bet she asks about the wedding.

"How did yesterday go?"

I knew it.

"I couldn't find my way here," she says. "Didn't they serve coffee?"

"Nope. Lemonade."

"That must have been tough on Mrs. Lucas. She rivaled me in the number of cups she drank a day."

"Yeah."

My mom sniffs a couple of times. "I bet you and Sam looked great."

"Sam looked good. I looked like a dork."

"Oh, Sherry, I'm sure that's not true." She sighs. "I really wanted to see you two dressed up."

I feel a tickle like a cotton ball or feather brushing my cheek. It's Mom. She's right by me. I close my eyes and just feel. I concentrate really hard. There's a sensation of pressure, like she's rubbing my shoulders. Then the light, feathery feeling again, but this time under my chin.

"Is this a rash?"

"Yeah. From stress, apparently."

"Makes sense," she says. "The wedding, the mystery challenge, probably some school worries in there somewhere. Anything else?" She pauses, and I can imagine her narrowing her eyes the way she used to when she was thinking hard. "And you're probably even more interested in boys now."

Ack. "No, no, no," I say, "everything's chill. I mean, other than the stuff you mentioned. Because that stuff is way stressful." My babbling won't stop. It's like my mouth is on fast-forward. "Stressful wedding, stressful mystery challenge, stressful boys. Yuppers. You name it, it's—"

"What's going on, Sherry?"

I am such a lousy liar. "Nothing, nothing, nothing. Every-thing's chill, chill, chi—"

"Don't tell me you and Junie had a fight. You two have been friends for a long time. And I count on Junie to keep you grounded."

"Oh, Mom." I roll my eyes. "Junie and me are good. We're always good." And in my relief at not having to lie, I say too much. "She totally gets my anxiety about—" I bite my tongue. Hard.

"Your anxiety about what?"

"Nothing." I swallow. Hard.

"Your anxiety about what?" Mom asks again, her voice low and even.

"It's not my fault," I wail. "You know what I'm like. It's unfair to dump a mystery on someone who sucks at challenges."

"What. Does. Junie. Know."

"Everything. She knows everything." My chin hits my chest. "I'm sorry. I couldn't help it."

Silence. A colossally enormous, scary silence.

chapter

13

It's afternoon, and I'm at the airport with my dad. It's like our school cafeteria: crowded and echoey-noisy, with too many different smells all jumbled together.

I've already checked in and am clutching my A boarding pass. My dad explained the whole system to me. On Southwest, you don't get assigned a seat but get herded onto the plane with everyone in your group, A, B or C. The As go first. The earlier you arrive at the airport, the more likely you are to snag an A, and then you have a better chance at snagging the seat of your choice.

We're waiting for Junie and Amber. Dad keeps checking his watch the way people jab repeatedly at the elevator button. He's sweating it because he has stuff to do before his and The

Ruler's flight later this afternoon. Like chauffeuring Sam to Grandma Baldwin's.

People are now walking around with B passes. Yikes. Where are Junie and Amber? I absolutely, positively must sit by Junie, so that we can work on a strategy for saving the rhinos. According to my mother, I really messed up big this time.

Apparently, now that Junie's in on the whole ghost-Academy-mystery thing, my mom's study group can't help us out. Academy rules state that student ghosts are allowed only a certain number of helpers on their spiritual team, and mortal helpers count for more than ghost ones.

The stupid Academy uses a stupid system like stupid Weight Watchers points. I know all about those because when my mother did Weight Watchers, we all did Weight Watchers. Basically, Junie is worth an entire bucket of KFC. Plus mashed potatoes, gravy and four biscuits. By confiding in Junie, I used up all my mother's points. And then some. Which means no study group. Even if Junie backed out, which she obviously won't, we can't recoup the points.

The only possible loophole in the whole dumb point thing is my grandfather, because birds are freebies, like water and cabbage. But can Grandpa, with his ancient old wings, make it to San Diego? If he can't lead my mom there, how will she ever find her way?

Yuppers. I definitely need planning time with Junie. Especially now that I'm down to her, myself, hopefully my mom and maybe my grandfather. Of the four of us, Junie's the only one on honor roll. I'm hoping Amber tails some cute guy onto the plane and hangs out next to him. That'd leave me and Junie free to scheme without any Amber interruptions.

Dad looks at me tap-tapping my boarding pass on my wrist. He puts his hand over mine and stops the movement. "Worried about sitting alone?"

"Basically."

"They could've gotten their boarding passes online," he says. He squeezes my shoulder. "It'll work out, Sherry." He surveys the waiting area. "And there they are." He calls out to Junie's mom, "Over here, May."

Dodging people, she heads toward us while Junie and Amber go to a huge window overlooking the runway. I wave to Junie, but she doesn't see me and keeps on yakking to Amber. Weird. She's not normally chatty-chatty. That's more my role.

And Junie's wearing a new outfit: paisley capris and a fuchsia tie-at-the-waist blouse. Did she go shopping with Amber? I'm Junie's shopping buddy. Have been for, like, years. My heart skips a bunch of beats.

Dad glances at his watch for the million-and-first time. "Do you mind waiting to see the girls off, May?"

"No problem, Bob." She pops up her clip-on sunglasses. "It's the least I can do for our personal travel agent."

Dad pulls me in for a tight hug. "Take good care of yourself, pumpkin. I need you back safe and sound."

I actually tear up watching the familiar, dorky way he bounces on his feet as he hurries away. Up, down. Up, down. Dorkity dork.

Eyeing my face, May says, "From what Junie said, I was expecting much worse."

68

Thankyouverymuch, Junie. Speaking of which, where is she?

I look around. Shoulders touching, Amber and Junie are still at the window, watching planes land and take off. They're hanging out together? Am I in a parallel universe? My heart skips some more beats.

"Go join the girls." May gives me a little push.

I plod to the window.

They're both holding A boarding passes.

Phew.

Amber is clipping Junie's hair at the top of her head, so that they look more like sisters than cousins. Well, only from behind and only from the neck up. I'm not being mean, just honest. Their faces are totally different. Junie is freckle city, while Amber has perfect Snow White skin. And Junie outweighs Amber by about twenty pounds. Whatever. They're looking super chummy, and it doesn't feel good. In fact, I'm probably going to faint.

When I get near them, I say, "Hi." But it comes out as more of a whisper. Probably because I'm close to keeling over. Anyway, they don't hear me, so I raise my voice in fake-o cheerfulness and say, "Hi, guys."

They both turn around and toss off a hi that's definitely lacking in the enthusiasm department.

Amber says, "I wanna hit the gift shop before we board."

Junie turns to follow her.

Ack. Ack. Ack. "Uh, Junie? Can we talk?"

"Sure." She gestures with her head to the store aisle.

"Uh, privately?" Duh. Has she forgotten about my mother? And how we have a mystery to solve? Plus, I need to fill her in on the latest developments, like how my grandfather is the state bird and how Junie and I may be carrying out the bulk of the investigation.

She raises her eyebrows. Only the teeniest, tiniest fraction, but when you've known someone as long as I've known Junie, you know exactly where her eyebrows sit. She's mad at me about something. But what? It doesn't matter. I'll grovel and apologize and grovel some more. I so, so, so need her help to save my mom.

"I'm gettin' gum." Amber walks away.

The minute she's out of earshot, I start talking at freeway speed. "My grandfather, the one who died in a car accident, is actually a wren. And he's coming to San Diego to help us. Hopefully. And—"

Junie looks at me. "Enough. I don't want to hear any more."

My jaw hits the floor.

"Sherry, you're delusional."

Okay. I'm not exactly sure what that means, but I sense it's bad. "Huh?"

"You're unbalanced, not thinking clearly. I believe it would be healthiest if you didn't talk about your mother or ghosts or, apparently, even birds."

"But she needs us."

Junie holds up her hands like stop signs. "You need professional help."

"I need you!"

"Sherry." Junie's hands are still up. "We'll write to Dr. Phil after spring break."

"I know this all seems crazy. I get that. But I'm not crazy. I am

70

so not crazy." Desperation makes my voice crack, so I sound like half the boys in our class. "It's really important that you believe me, Junie."

Her eyes are unblinking and blank. She's not budging.

"It's you! The problem is you!" I stamp my foot. "You know what you are? You are stupid. Very, very stupid."

She goes all still except for her nostrils, which flare. Being smart is really important to Junie.

"You heard me. Stupid. Seriously stupid. Severely stupid. Just because the Academy of Spirits isn't in one of your textbooks doesn't mean it doesn't exist."

Suddenly the loudspeaker crackles. "All passengers holding A passes may now board the plane."

Junie looks down at my A pass.

I stare at her A pass.

Her face all red and shiny and her nostrils still flaring, Junie says, "Let's sit apart. We both need some time to cool off."

I am so dead in the water.

chapter 14

I spend the flight across the aisle and a few rows behind Junie and Amber. Heads together, they spend the flight talking and laughing and listening to each other's iPods. By the time our plane touches down in San Diego, I've figured out two important things.

First, I have to get along with them. I need Junie's brains, and I need Amber's driving abilities. *Plan:* I will blast Amber and Junie with megadoses of Sherry niceness.

Second, I gotta get my mom and grandfather out here. I might still be doomed with them, but I'm definitely doomed without them. *Plan:* I will blaze a caffeine trail for my mother. I will think of something to help Grandpa find me.

Shrugging on my backpack, I follow Amber and Junie off the

plane. In the terminal, Junie points to a sign showing the direction of the baggage-pickup area. By the time we get there, luggage from our flight is already riding around on the carousel.

"I see mine." Amber sashays toward a Silly Putty–pink suitcase. Within seconds, she's standing, a hip jutted out, while some guy hauls her bag off the conveyor belt.

Junie and me hang in silence, watching the carousel.

"Isn't that our luggage?" I say, ever the helpful friend.

"Thanks, Sherry." Junie's trying to get along too.

In a gentle arc, she glides her bag off the carousel.

Unfortunately, it takes me several tries to wrestle my suitcase into submission. I may have seriously overpacked. Panting, I finally get it upright and on its one remaining wheel. I stick out my lower lip and puff my bangs off my forehead.

Amber's staring at me like I'm contagious. Finally, she says, "Where's your aunt?"

I look around. "She must be here somewhere."

Amber frowns.

"What does she look like?" Junie asks.

I pause for a sec, narrowing down the description. "Geriatric."

"Fine," Amber says with a heavy, disgusted sigh, "let's see if we can find her."

We meander through the baggage-claim area. Amber and Junie lightly tug on their suitcases, which obey like well-trained dogs by rolling behind them in perfect straight lines. I alternately yank, push, kick and drag my crippled, misbehaving case. It wobbles all lopsided, attacking the ankles of all who stray into its crazed path.

"You have her phone number?" Junie asks.

"Great idea." I unzip my backpack, pull out my cell and turn it on. Stored in it is Great-aunt Margaret's number, along with numbers for my dad, The Ruler, Grandma Baldwin, Junie, Brianna, Kristin, Margo, Sara, and, of course, Josh. I am so loving having a cell phone.

Before I finish scrolling through the address book, my phone rings.

"It better be her." Amber scowls.

I look at the screen. Dad. I flip open the phone. "We can't find Great-aunt Margaret."

"And you won't," he says. "She's at the hospital with her best friend, a sorority sister from decades ago, who fell down and broke a hip."

"What about us?"

"Take a taxi to the condo. Your aunt's going to stay at her friend's place to help when she gets out of the hospital. Just for a few days. Just until the daughter gets into town." Dad pauses, probably to crack his knuckles. "Margaret seems to think you three will be okay. She left her car for Amber. I don't know, though. I could call Southwest and see about bringing you all back here today."

Ah. It is tempting to fly back to Phoenix, away from my woeful woes with Amber and Junie and toward blissful bliss with Josh. But, no, no, no, there's the huge issue of my mother's afterlife. "It's chill, Dad."

"I'm not sure what I'd do with you here, anyway. Paula and I are

74

at the airport, waiting to board," he says. "I'm worried your grandmother's starting to lose it. She's obsessed about some bird that hasn't been to her feeder today."

I pump the air with a victory fist. Yes, yes, yes! Who knew I'd feel such joy and relief at the thought of a plump, balding old wren flapping out to meet me?

He goes on to give me detailed instructions about taking a taxi, paying for it with money he gave me and touching base daily with my great-aunt. Then he makes sure I have her address and tells me where the front-door key is hidden. Finally he winds up the call with how much he loves me and a reminder to use common sense.

"Ditto," I say. I'm just about to snap my phone closed, when he calls my name.

"That was a really nice thing you did for Sam, giving him your mother's afghan to take to Grandma's."

"Yeah, well," I say, "whatever. He *is* feeding my fish for me." I go to hang up and Dad calls my name again. It's like he can't let me off the phone.

"I almost forgot. Margaret said she left something fun for you guys on the kitchen counter."

"Groovy," I say, and disconnect.

"What's going on?" Junie asks.

Amber's tapping her foot.

I fill them in.

"Maybe she left us party supplies," Amber says.

"I kind of doubt it," I say. In an effort to remain nice, I do not call her an idiot.

Amber spins around, doing syllable hand claps. "Par-ty, par-ty."

Junie herds us out of the baggage area and toward the exit, where we join the cab line. The whole time, Amber's running off at the mouth about guys and parties. Junie and me are quiet. I don't know where Junie's head's at, but I'm stressing to the max. Because now, Great-aunt Margaret won't be giving me even one single ride to the Wild Animal Park.

I'm totally dependent on Amber.

chapter 15

"Just a sec!" I yell over my shoulder, while racing back into the arrivals building. Into the newsstand store. Over to the cash register. I know exactly what I want. Where is it? Where is it?

Head swiveling and eyes scanning, I'm like Robocop, only way better-looking. Left, right. Up, down. Listerine strips. Certs. Altoids. Talk about your national bad-breath crisis. Still looking. Still looking. It's gotta be here. We cannot miss our taxi turn because of me.

Ah-ha. There it is, hanging from a silver hook. I snatch a package, throw some money on the counter, then zip back to the taxi stand.

Amber and Junie are tossing their bags into the trunk of a waiting cab.

Junie eyes what I'm carrying, then silently points to my suit-case, which lies like roadkill on the sidewalk.

Amber's eyebrows are plucked into the shape of McDonald's arches. Now she raises them really high, practically to her hair-line, and shoots me a killer look of disdain. "You rushed off for sunflower seeds?"

"Well, yeah."

"Sherry," Amber says as we all pile into the backseat, "quit be-ing such a weirdo."

I don't answer. There's really no response to such rudeness.

The cabdriver, a woman, slams down the trunk, then hops in the car and resets the meter.

I rattle off my great-aunt's address on Coronado Island.

"Welcome to America's Finest City." The driver clicks on her signal.

Amber takes out a thick, striped emery board and goes to work on her left hand.

Junie stares out the window.

I fiddle with the sunflower-seed package.

We nose into the carpool lane and head over the Coronado-Bay Bridge. "Look off in the distance," the driver says. "See the white building with the red roof and turrets? That's the Hotel del Coronado—the Del, to us natives. Your condo's down the beach from it." She brakes at a stop sign. "They're filming a murder mys-tery between your condo and the Del."

Amber stops filing and leans forward. "Who's in it?"

The driver taps her fingers on the dash. "The guy from *Death for Two*. And—"

"Damon Walker!" Amber squeals. "I'm still in shock he didn't get an Oscar for *Death for Two*."

Say what? He wasn't even nominated. Because he's a bad, bad actor. Shoulda-stuck-with-modeling bad.

"Who else? Who else?" Amber bounces on the seat like she just swigged a two-liter bottle of Coke. "Who else is in the movie?"

"I can't remember the name of the actress." The driver switches lanes. "She hasn't been in much. I know she did a documentary in Africa." She looks in the rearview mirror. "Something to do with rhinos and extinction."

I sit up straight.

"Kendra Phillips?" Junie asks, the resident public-TV viewer.

The driver snaps her fingers. "Kendra Phillips. Yup. That's the one."

For the rest of the ride, the driver indicates places of interest. I barely listen; all the little rhino connections are jumbled up in my mind like some bizarre dot-to-dot.

When we get to the condo, I find the fake rock my dad described and reach inside it for the key. Bingo. In the dusk, though, I have trouble fitting the key into the lock.

Behind me, Amber groans.

"Let me try," Junie says.

I hand her the key and wait while she slides it in and turns. She pushes open the door and steps back to let me enter first.

I feel along the wall for the light switch and flip it on.

Gasp.

Gasp.

Gasp.

That's a gasp from each of us.

The entryway is totally pink: ceiling, walls, tiles. We venture down the hall into the living room to discover more of the same: pink furniture, pink lamps, pink cushions. It's like we're trapped in a giant Dubble Bubble bubble.

"What kinda freakin' genius lives here?" Amber smacks her forehead.

"The Pink Panther." Junie flops down on the pink couch. "I feel queasy."

"I love it." Amber dances around the room, oohing and ahhing. "Check this out." She rubs a lamp. "It's the exact shade of cotton candy. And dusty rose carpet, flamingo walls. Incredible."

Junie closes her eyes. Her face is Shrek green.

Amber reads aloud from a coral wall plaque, " 'Pink Lady Award, Margaret Jackson of San Diego County, Most Mary Kay Sales After the Age of Seventy.' " She whistles. "Very cool."

"You love all this?" I ask Amber. "For real?" I can't read this girl.

"Yes." She sighs. "What a great surprise."

"This isn't the surprise. It's supposed to be on the counter."

Amber and I head over to the (yes, pink) counter to find a (yes, pink) envelope with *Girls* written on it.

Amber rips open the envelope. She pulls out a bunch of tickets, glances at them, then tosses them up in the air. As they feather-float to the carpet, she announces, "They're all yours, Sherry."

I kneel to pick them up. Beige passes to the Wild Animal Park.

"I'm starving," Amber announces.

"I can't eat here," Junie says. "Much more time in this Pepto-Bismol pit, and I'll throw up."

"How about the Hotel Del?" I suggest. "They gotta have a restaurant or something."

So the three of us end up walking along the beach toward the hotel.

"What a spectacular view." Eyes wide, Junie ogles the horizon.

Yowser. Wowser. Personally, I'm not much into nature. Well, except for boys. But the sunset *is* totally awesome. The sun looks like a huge golden jawbreaker hanging in a purple-and-orange-striped sky. We stand there, gazing. Then, all of a sudden, the sun dippity-dips into the ocean. And, gulp, it's swallowed up.

The beach is dimmer now, with only a little light spilling onto the shore from nearby hotels and condos. I breathe through my mouth to avoid the yucko smell of salt water and seaweed.

"I'll meet you guys there." And Amber takes off.

Lips turned down, Junie watches her cousin. "I guess she's afraid we'll cramp her style." She walks over to a rock and sits. She wiggles her fingers in a shallow tide pool. "Brrrr. This water is frigid."

I perch on a boulder beside her. I kick off my sandals. In the damp sand, my fluorescent-mulberry toenails glitter like gems.

We sit quietly, side by side. Niceness vibes are oozing out of my pores like sweat on a hundred-degree day. I'm truly the perfect example of an easy-to-get-along-with friend. The type of friend you want to solve a mystery with to save her ghost mother from being expelled from the Academy of Spirits.

A male voice pierces my thoughts. "You can't go to the Wild Animal Park tomorrow. I need you here, Kendra."

I squint into the dark. Silhouetted against the night sky, a guy and girl are meandering along. They stop about twenty feet from us.

The girl says gently, "But, Damon, I'm the rhino spokesperson. And tomorrow is the Save the Rhinos ceremony."

Damon? As in Damon Walker? I squint harder. He's even better-looking in real life. He's tall. He's gorgeous. He's the kind of guy you want taped to your bedroom door. A poster of him, that is.

Standing beside Damon is a girl who must be Kendra Phillips. I've never seen her in anything. She's pretty, with shoulder-length reddish hair. But he totally, totally outshines her in the beauty department.

The couple begins strolling again, then stops. Right in front of us. It's like me and Junie have front-row seats to *The Damon and Kendra Show*. I freeze, trying to shadow-meld into a boulder.

Kendra says, "And Gina hasn't had her calf yet. Sue called me today, and it doesn't look as though it's going to happen tonight."

"Who's Sue?"

"You know. The head rhino keeper?"

"I don't keep track of your rhino friends." Damon shrugs. "Quite frankly, I'm tired of always coming in second to them and those animals."

"That's not fair." She reaches out to touch him, but he steps back.

"This movie's very important to me," Damon says. "I really want you on the set tomorrow when I do the stunts."

Kendra looks down. "I'm not in any scenes until the end of the week. It won't affect the shoot at all if I'm at the Park."

"Be honest." Damon's arms thump to his side. "You never wanted to do this picture. You think you're too good for it." He runs his fingers through his hair. "Maybe we should take a break from each other when we're finished with this flick."

82

Kendra's face turns glow-in-the-dark white. "You mean a lot to me, Damon," she says with a catch in her voice. "But I have a commitment to the Park too. Let's talk later, when we're both less emotional." She turns and tramps away, head down and shoulders slumped.

He watches her for a moment, kicks the sand hard, like he's trying to toe-dig to China, then storms off in the opposite direction.

I let out a breath I didn't even realize I was holding.

"What a jerk," Junie says. "Amber's mother was married to a guy like that for a while. He always threatened to leave when he didn't get his own way. Then one day he did leave. It was really tough on Amber."

I feel bad for Kendra. For Amber too. Almost.

We follow in Kendra's footsteps. She's ahead on the beach, shoulders still rounded.

Junie glances over at me. "Your rash is gone."

I run my fingertips along my chin and neck. Beautifully bumpless. "Yay."

"Your skin looks good."

And then, because we're sharing a friendly moment and because I've been incredibly nice and likable, I open my big, fat mouth. "Did you hear how rhino stuff came up again?"

"Don't start with me, Sherry." Junie picks up the pace.

Fine. Just poke me in the eye with a piñata stick.

Junie and I plod along the beach, not speaking. Eventually, we meet up with a sidewalk that winds past lit tennis courts and dumps us in front of a Hotel Del Café sign. A crimson painted arrow indicates the restaurant is at the top of some wooden steps. We start climbing.

At the landing, we're greeted by an incredibly adorable waiter in a white apron over a charcoal T-shirt and shorts.

"Good evening, ladies." He smiles with big dimples. "Are you here with Amber?"

"Y-y-yes," Junie stammers.

I mean, she actually stammers. What's that all about? And she's gawking at him. The kind of gawking she usually saves for the computer aisle at Fry's Electronics.

"Follow me," he says.

High above the dim, dank beach, the restaurant is an oasis of light, heat and delish food smells. I salivate as we wend our way to Amber.

She queen-waves at us from across the room, where she's not sitting alone but with a dark-haired cutie-pie. That girl does not waste time.

Junie slides into a chair next to Amber, and I sit beside Junie.

Amber points a glittery fake nail at the waiter. "This is Ben. He's a college student at San Diego State. He works here part-time and surfs when he gets the chance.

"And this is Rob." She squeezes the arm of the cutie-pie. "Rob's a reporter. Real important at the newspaper where he works. Lives alone."

Excuse me. Did I make a wrong turn and wind up on the set of some tacky cable dating show?

Amber nods in our direction. "This is my little cousin, Junie, and her little friend Sherry."

Major gag.

Junie crosses her arms and zings daggerish looks at Amber.

Ben pulls a pad and pen from the front pocket of his apron and says to me and Junie, "Something to drink?"

"We'll take a pitcher of Coke," Amber says.

I want to slap that bossy girl. Instead I contradict her. "Sprite for me."

"Me too," Junie says.

"I'll be right back," Ben says, then looks at Amber. "Let me check on the nachos."

She tilts her head to the side, her straight blond hair swaying. "Okay, Ben." She turns to us little people. "I ordered a huge plate of deluxe nachos."

My stomach grumbles.

Junie gapes at Ben like she's stranded in the desert and he's a bottle of sparkling water.

Rob clears his throat. "I write for *the* San Diego daily paper—the *Union-Tribune*." He straightens the collar of his short-sleeved white button-down. "Or the *Trib,* as we say in the biz."

He looks young to be a reporter. Like in his twenties. And, while he's extremely gorgeous, I can't help but notice that his thick hair is overgelled. I give a subtle sniff. A little too flowery.

Rob gazes at Amber. "Which college did you say you're at?"

"I live in Phoenix," Amber answers.

From the ease with which she sidesteps the college-student-versus-only-a-high-school-student question, I'm betting Amber has navigated these waters before. She probably even has fake ID.

She flutters her eyelashes. "You, like, got any suggestions for what we should do while we're here?"

Rob rattles off a bunch of stuff.

With a sideways glance at me, Amber says, "Why didn't you mention the Wild Animal Park?"

"Because it's a total drag." Rob slurps a few sips from his hot chocolate. "You just can't compare a couple thousand acres of dirt and boring animals with beaches, shopping and great restaurants."

It strikes me that Rob's forehead is too large. Almost cartoonish.

"What about the rhino baby?" I ask.

"It's a rhino"—he hikes his eyebrows up into the huge desert of his forehead—"having a calf." He raises them some more. "You only have a week in San Diego. I live here, and I wouldn't waste my time at the Park."

Ben interrupts Rob's rhino bashing with a humongous platter of nachos. There's silence while we all dig in.

A giant chip loaded with refried beans and cheese between my fingers, I tip back in my plastic chair and scope out the area. Except for us, the café is empty. A few tables over, a tall, aluminum outdoor heater blasts warmth.

I can see over the metal rail to the dark shore below. Waves are crashing, and there's a small knot of people milling about. I shift my gaze to the tennis courts.

Flash.

Say what? I peer at the courts.

Flash.

Someone's hiding down there.

chapter

16

I set down the chip and stand right next to the rail for a better view.

"What are you doing, Sherry?" Junie turns in her chair. Her voice is scratchy-irritated.

"Someone's on the courts. What's he holding that just glinted?"

Amber rolls her eyes.

Rob jumps up and joins me. As he pulls his hands from his pockets to grip the rail, a small piece of paper flutters to the floor.

I step on it.

He's totally fixated on the beach scene, his stare jumping between the courts and the group of people.

I bend down, fake-adjust the strap on my sandal and snatch up the paper. A torn entrance ticket to the Wild Animal Park. Huh?

So, he does go to the Park. But he doesn't want us to go. Why? Does he know what's going on up there? Is he involved? I poke the ticket into my pocket.

Flash.

Junie pushes her glasses higher up on her nose and squints into the darkness. "Binoculars."

"Probably a bird-watcher." Rob's knuckles are white.

Amber gets up and leans into Rob, her hip against his. She fluffs her hair. "Boring."

Birds? No way. It's either us or those people. "I'm going down to check it out," I say.

Junie shakes her head. She totally thinks I've lost it.

"I'll go," Rob says.

Amber loops her arm through his. "No, you won't."

Before he answers, I take off, zigzagging around the tables until I reach the exit. Then I crouch and creep down the steps. When I get to the bottom, I sit, leaning into the fence and the thick honeysuckle growing up it. What a sickly-sweet smell.

Through a gap in the green leaves and yellow flowers, I focus on a figure kneeling in the shadow of the tennis net. He's short, with messy orange hair and freakishly long arms. All rigid, he's holding binoculars up to his eyes. The binoculars are trained on the group on the beach.

I turn my attention to the people standing and chatting on the sand just beyond the cement walkway. Damon Walker's there!

What are they saying? Crawling next to the fence, I'm shaky and wobbly. Like the first time you roll out of bed after the flu. This PI lifestyle is stressful.

A swift peek back at the courts tells me Monkey Man's still glued to his binoculars.

Damon barks out, "Where's Kendra? Why isn't she chilling with the rest of us?"

Silence. Everyone examines their feet.

It's at this very intense moment that my cell phone chooses to ring.

chapter 17

Ring. Ring. Ring.

All eyes in the group shift to me.

Ring. Ring. Ring.

Yikes. Yikes. Yikes.

How long before my voice mail picks up? What did The Ruler set it at? July?

I jerk my mini-backpack off and try to unzip it to get to the phone. The zipper is stuck. I yank and pull on it. Nada.

Ring. Ring. Ring.

Then I try feeling for the phone through the canvas material so I can push the disconnect button. My backpack is full of nothing but phonelike lumps. I jab, jab, jab on everything.

Finally, the ringing stops.

All eyes are still staring at me. Time feels stretched out like a rubber band.

On the tennis courts, Monkey Man lowers his binoculars and focuses on me like he's memorizing my face. Then, with his apelike arms, he shoves open the gate to the courts and bolts off down the beach, clouds of sand kicking up behind him.

Damon watches, frowning and stroking his chin. If this were a comic book, Damon would have a question-mark bubble above his head. It looks like a thousand thoughts are fighting for space in his brain. And I don't mean nice, pleasant thoughts.

Damon turns and aims his famous pistachio green eyes at me, probably trying to figure out where I fit into the mysterious-guy-with-binoculars puzzle. And I know in my churning gut that I don't want Damon to associate me with Monkey Man.

I twirl a bunch of hair around my finger. Then suddenly—and who knows where the brilliant idea pops in from—I say, "Can I have your autograph?"

There's more silence, like he needs time to switch gears. Then, smiling with perfect, pearly teeth, he stretches out a hand. "Sure."

Huh? Oh, I get it. I dig in the outside pocket of my backpack and come up with a pen and my boarding pass. I hand them over.

Damon leans against his thigh to write. He doesn't even ask my name. And in the middle of scrawling "Walker," he glances back at his friends. "Come on, guys. We have a big day tomorrow."

After they're gone, I unhook the latch on the gate to the courts. Maybe Monkey Man left behind a clue. I shuffle over to where he was kneeling. What am I stepping on? I bend down and grab up . . . I don't know what, exactly. Some weird mixture of seeds and pellets. There's a small pile and then a thin trail leading to the gate. Looks like Monkey Man has a hole in his pocket.

Is he carrying around a healthy California snack? I sniff. I cough. Yuckerama. It stinks like cat food. No way I'm tasting that. Then a bizarre, way-out-there thought hits me. Could this strange, smelly stuff possibly be poison? Rhino poison? I push a handful of it down into my pocket. I'll show it to my mother. If she shows up.

I jog back up the steps. All this physical exercise must be toning me for the beach. As I thread through the restaurant, I can see Amber and Junie wolfing down nachos.

Rob's sitting still, his eyes on me, his fingers drumming the table.

Junie asks, all critical, "What were you doing on the tennis courts?"

Rob stops drumming.

"Just looking," I answer slowly. I don't trust Rob. He totally lied about going to the Wild Animal Park. I have no idea why, but he did. Which makes him a liar with a wide forehead and too much hair gel.

"What was on the ground?" Rob asks.

I shrug. "Nothing, really. Sand. Dirt. The usual."

Amber stops inhaling food. "Did Damon Walker actually talk to you? *The* Damon Walker?"

I nod. "Here." I slide the boarding pass across the table. Bribery for her chauffeuring skills. "You can have his autograph."

"Wow." With the pad of her index finger, she traces over Damon's signature. "Thanks, Sherry. You know, you're pretty cool, considering you're delusional."

My breath catches in my throat. "Delusional" is so not an Amber word. "Delusional" is a Junie word. What exactly did Junie blab to Amber about me?

Junie concentrates on her napkin, twisting it tighter and tighter. Her gazillion freckles pop out all 3-D.

Elbows on the table, and chin propped on the bridge formed by his hands, Rob watches me. His eyes flick to Junie, then to Amber, then to me again.

Amber flips her hair back. "Like, about the rhinos."

Help. I know I should do something, react somehow. Instead I totally freeze.

"Amber." Junie glares.

"What? Like it's not whacked to be all worried someone's trying to kill the rhinos at the Wild Animal Park?" Then, exaggerating every sound like I'm suddenly from Russia or somewhere, Amber says, "You need help. Rob says there's medication for people like you."

Rob says? Double help. Amber blabbed to Rob.

"Ouch." Amber frowns at Junie. "That was my shin. And you know I bruise easy." She swings a leg out from under the table and begins rubbing it. "Sherry, I just wanna say it's pretty scary how fast you've gone downhill."

I'm breathing through my nostrils because I can't even get my mouth open. Forget about telling her to shut up.

Statue still, Rob's taking in the whole scene.

Amber straightens her too-tight T-shirt. "Do yourself a favor and lose the 'I gotta help my mom, the ghost in trouble' act. You're the one who needs help, and soon."

"Amber, shut up," Junie says.

Somehow Amber pairing "lose" with "my mom" is what finally spurs me to action. I spring to my feet and race like I'm running for my life across the restaurant, down the steps and onto the beach.

Bent in half like a pretzel and hands clamped on my knees, I suck in raggedy breaths of salty night air.

After a while, I see Junie powering toward me.

"Sherry!" She waves her arms above her head. "Sherry!" She huffs and puffs.

I straighten. Here it comes: the Big Apology.

"Look." Junie toes the sand. "I didn't mean for that to happen."

No duh. Usually when you blab a friend's important and sensitive secrets, you don't mean for her to find out.

"But we're, uh, all here together for a week. And we'll have more fun if we, uh, get along." With the back of her hand, Junie wipes sweat off her blotchy forehead. "I think it'll work if we just don't mention the rhinos or, uh, other stuff." She pauses. "Okay?"

My face must show how pathetic I think she sounds, because she rushes into, "Rob can get us on the movie set tomorrow morning as extras. We'll get to see Damon Walker doing his own water-skiing stunt."

Tomorrow morning? No. No. No. That's when the rhino ceremony is, at the Park. I have to be there. And Amber has to drive me. Solving this mystery is turning into a humongous headache.

I'm so caught up in stress and worry, I don't really hear Junie until she taps my shoulder.

"Sherry, on the beach, why were they all staring at you?"

"My phone rang." My phone rang. I can't believe I forgot. I plop down on the walkway, yank off my backpack. This time the zipper whips open like it's been greased. Whatever.

I click on Calls Missed. "Josh Morton" pops up on the screen. Josh Morton called me!

My hand slaps over my chest to prevent my thumping heart from leaping out onto the sand.

A quick click on the flashing envelope and I'm listening to his message. "I got your number from Kristin. I have some news I think you'll like. At least, I hope so. Call me."

"Josh wants me to call him." I swing my backpack over my shoulder. "Catch you later." I stand and walk away from Junie and her round-like-Frisbees eyes.

It's dark now, with dim lights from the condo casting long shadows out to sea. Crashing waves beat up the shore.

I find a patch of dry ground not too close to stinky seaweed and sit. Inhaling a bunch of salty air, I flip open my phone and dial Josh.

I put the phone to my ear. With the first ring, my stomach flip-flops. With the second ring, it flop-flips. With the third, fourth and fifth rings, it's all over the place, doing its gymnastic thing.

Josh's voice mail picks up. My stomach stops mid flip. Voice mail? Wah.

I listen to his message, storing it in my memory right next to his phone number: "This is Josh. Leave a message. Later, dude."

"Hi, uh, Josh. Sorry I didn't answer. I was, uh, at the beach. By the Hotel Del. Call me." I snap the phone shut and put it away. Okay. I just sounded dumb.

I'm so into worrying about my lame message, then wondering what Josh's news is, that it takes me a minute to realize a fatty cactus wren has landed on my shoulder. He curls his feet into my sweater.

"Grandpa!" My spirits soar at the sight of him. "Where's Mom?"

He looks down the beach, lifts one foot and holds it above his eyes.

I squint into the darkness. "Was she far behind you? Is she on her way?"

He bobs his head.

I feel in my backpack for the package of sunflower seeds I bought at the airport. Once my palm is full, I stick out my arm. Grandpa hops down the length of it and onto my outstretched finger.

Peck. Peck. Peck. He is seriously munching down.

I watch the beach for any sign of movement, sniffing for coffee. Suddenly I see a colossal cloud of sand swirling near the waves. Swirling fast. Swirling wild. And swirling right for me.

chapter 18

"Grandpa," I yell, "tell Mom to slow down!"

Peck. Peck. Peck. He's going jackhammer speed on the seeds. He doesn't pause, doesn't look up, just tightens his grip on my finger. Ouch.

The cloud's barreling closer and closer, churning out sand from the sides.

"Slow down!" I scream.

Mom's still racing. And now I can hear her too, like wind whooshing through a tunnel.

I jump up, hold Grandpa in safe to my chest and start dancing from side to side, trying to dodge her. But she's not traveling in a straight line. She's, like, Queen Zigzag of the Sand Cyclones.

I stop dancing. This is totally useless. I can't outmaneuver her.

Legs apart, I turn my back, dig my toes into the sand and squeeze my eyes shut. "Hang on for your life, Grandpa."

I'm standing tough, knees bent and shoulders hunched. My hair and clothes blow crazy on one side, like I'm next to the summer fan display at Home Depot.

Then all goes quiet. All goes still.

I open my eyes. A few grains of sand are popping around next to my feet. There's a coffee smell in the air.

"Whew," Mom says. "Sand is a tough traveling medium."

"You almost killed us." I unfold my arms. "Grandpa, are you okay?"

Balanced on my wrist, he pecks at my empty palm.

I pull the sunflower-seed package out of my backpack and dump the rest in my hand.

He goes back to munching and crunching.

"How thoughtful of you, Sherry," Mom says.

I shrug. "Yeah, well, I thought the seeds would help Grandpa find me. Turns out he didn't need them; he flew to me all on his own."

"Your grandfather's an excellent navigator. Thanks to him, we're here and off to a successful start. What have you been up to?"

Grandpa swallows the last seed and scratches my wrist.

I reach into my backpack and glide the crystal out. "Grandma gave me this."

Grandpa rubs his head on it, cooing. Very cute and romantic.

Then I fill them in on Monkey Man and his weird seedy-pellety stuff; and Rob the Reporter, who really doesn't want us to visit the Wild Animal Park; and Kendra, official rhino spokesperson, and her beach argument with Damon.

"Good work, Sherry," Mom says. "Let's see the seed mixture from the tennis courts."

With my free hand, I pull some out of my pocket.

Quicker than you can say "Don't eat the evidence," Grandpa leaps over to my palm and starts noshing.

"Grandpa, stop." I close my hand. "It might be poison."

He shakes his head and beak-pokes my fist.

"She's got a point, Wilhelm," Mom says. "Sherry, let me see it."

I open my palm flat. A warm, gentle breeze whispers over it, gently blowing the seeds and pellets around. My throat lumps up. My mom is touching me.

The breeze stops, and my hand goes all chilly. "I'm not sure what it is," Mom says. "Put it in a Ziploc bag at the condo. And make sure you wash your hands."

Grandpa fluffs up his scraggly feathers and squawks, "Bye."

At least, I think it was "bye." Coulda been "pie." Maybe "spy." Or "my."

Then he spreads his wings and takes off into the night, turning into a tiny irregularly shaped dot lit up by the condo lights.

I say, "That was abrupt." I push the seedy-pellety stuff back into my pocket and put the crystal away.

"Grandpa's not really himself right now," Mom says. "The trip tired him out. Plus, he's upset about Grandma. He didn't want to leave her, and he's worried that's she's worried because he's suddenly not showing up at her feeder."

"Why didn't he tell her where he was going?"

She coughs. "Grandma's not as open to us as she'd like to think."

My jaw drops. "No way. I can tap into the spirit world, and Grandma can't?" I've got a special spiritual talent that my Birkenstock-wearing, incense-burning, crystal-dangling grandmother doesn't. I puff out my chest.

"Where'd Grandpa go?"

"He's staying at a hostel for spirit animals."

"How about you?"

"The Whaley House, in Old Town. It's very popular with ghosts."

Probably the haunted house Josh mentioned. "Do you really need to stay anywhere? I mean, you're a ghost."

"I like the camaraderie. And for me, it's safer because I can't just float off."

The extreme weirdness in my life continues. "How are you gonna get there?"

"The same way I got out here. Your grandfather"—she pauses—" 'maps' the way."

It takes me a sec to get what Mom's saying. "Ew. Ew. Ew." I stick out my tongue in true grossed-out-edness. "He makes you a trail of bird poop?"

"It works." She clears her throat, a let's-get-down-to-business sound. "Sherry, we need to get to the Wild Animal Park ASAP. As in tomorrow."

"It's a problem." A chilly night wind blasts down the beach. I button my sweater. I tell her about Junie blabbing to Amber, how they're going to a movie shoot tomorrow and how Great-aunt Margaret can't drive me because of her sick friend.

"There must be something. . . ."

I bet she's twirling her hair around a finger, thinking away.

My phone rings. I slide it out of my pocket and glance at the screen. Josh. And even though I've been waiting for this call since September, I slide the phone, unanswered, back in my pocket.

Ring. Ring. Ring.

"You don't want to get that?" Mom asks.

Ring. Ring. Ring.

"I'll call back later." Sometimes the boy has to wait. Like when you're working on a mystery. Like when your mother's right there, so you wouldn't have any privacy. "About getting to the Park—maybe there's a bus? Or a shuttle from the hotel?"

"And try Amber again," Mom says. "Then coffee-call me tomorrow."

And, poof, she's gone. No more smell of coffee. No more sand activity.

No more making the boy wait.

Surf pounding on the beach, pulse pounding in my ears, I call Josh.

"Guess what?" he says. "I'm flying to San Diego on Thursday. It's a surprise reward for doing so good on my report card."

I squeal. Literally. Very uncool.

"I'll be staying at my cousins', but we can definitely hook up."

Hook up? My stomach switches places with my liver. "Sick."

We disconnect, and I slowly return my cell to my mini-backpack. Josh is coming to San Diego and wants to spend time with me. Awesome. But how will I juggle him and the mystery?

A full moon has risen, a sugar cookie in the night sky. I stare at the round, glowing ball and think. Basically, there's only one solution.

I have to wrap up the mystery really, really fast.

Dark clouds pass in front of the moon. One looks like a Popsicle. Brrrr. One looks like a, well, a shapeless cloud. And one looks like a rhino.

I snap my fingers. I just might know how to get to the Park tomorrow.

It's around eight o'clock at night, and I'm standing in front of the reservations desk at the Hotel Del. I clear my throat.

Behind the counter, a short-haired middle-aged man looks up at me. "Just a minute." He shuffles a few more papers. "Are you looking for the free-ice-cream vouchers?"

"No." I draw a deep, deep breath. "I'd like to speak with Kendra Phillips."

He stares down his long nose. "I don't think so."

I look at the gold nameplate pinned to his stiff white shirt. "Mr. Lopez, could you please tell Kendra Phillips that Sue from the Wild Animal Park is here?"

He narrows his eyes. "Sue? From the Wild Animal Park?"

I nod. I'm sweating buckets.

After checking his computer monitor, he picks up the phone and jabs in some numbers. "Ms. Phillips? A Sue from the Wild Animal Park is here to see you." He pauses. "Oh really? Yes, I'll tell her."

Mr. Lopez straightens his tie. "Sue, Ms. Phillips will be right down." He points to a couch by the elevators. "You can wait over there."

"Thank you." I smile like I'm used to getting past obnoxious hotel clerks and chilling with actresses.

I skip over to the leather couch and plop down. The coffee table in front of me gives off a whiff of furniture polish.

My plan is working. Of course, I'm not Sue, and I'm not from the Wild Animal Park. But I haven't crashed and burned yet.

The elevator doors open. Kendra steps out and glances around. She's wearing sweats and a frayed Old Navy T-shirt. Not overly Hollywoodish.

I get up and walk toward her. "Hi, I'm Sherry Baldwin."

Kendra looks puzzled. "Where's Sue?"

"Well, she's not exactly here."

Her forehead wrinkles. "Is she on her way?"

"Well, not exactly."

"What's going on?" Kendra crosses her arms.

"I want to help with the rhinos."

"Okay," she says slowly. "You can come to the Wild Animal Park tomorrow for the Save the Rhinos ceremony. And you can donate online." Kendra pauses. "How old are you?"

"Thirteen."

"Your parents can donate for you."

Like she's that old. Now that I'm up close to her in a lighted place, I can see she's probably older than Amber, but not by much. She's maybe twenty. And not that I'll ever mention it, but Kendra's left eye's a little smaller than her right one. She's still really cute and all, just not symmetrical.

"Nice meeting you." Kendra heads toward the elevators.

Ack. My best shot at getting to the Park is walking away. I gulp air like a fish out of water. "I know about the extra bananas left for the rhinos."

She stops and turns back to me. "How? That info was never released to the public."

"A guy who knows a guy who knows a snitch. Typical informer situation."

"What?" she says, looking all confused. "What's your name again?"

"Sherry Baldwin." I start talking a mile a minute. "I really am worried about the rhinos. And, like I just told you, I'm only thirteen, which means I can't drive. I'm in San Diego for spring break, staying at my great-aunt's. But she can't drive me because she's looking after a sick friend. And I desperately need a ride to the Park tomorrow. And I know you're going because I overheard you and Damon Walker on the beach earlier." Oops. That last part just kinda slipped out.

Kendra goes red. "You're right. I am going tomorrow."

"The rhinos need all the help they can get," I say, "what with extinction and all." And then I yak about the Phoenix Zoo, where I had my second-grade birthday party, where you can camp overnight, where they put up a bajillion lights over the holidays. Basically, I just babble on and on, talking fast, barely breathing. This strategy works great with my dad.

After about five minutes, Kendra's eyes glaze over. "Okay, okay. What does your great-aunt say about you riding with me?"

Bingo. I whip out my phone, call my aunt and spill. She asks to talk with Kendra. I cross my fingers and ankles for good luck while she grills Kendra for about three years, practically asking for reference letters and baby pics.

"No, I've never tried Mary Kay makeup," Kendra says, then listens for a second. "That'd be great. Bye." Kendra passes me the phone. "Your aunt says to use one of the free passes."

I nod in a cool way, but inside I'm pogo-sticking. It worked. My plan totally worked.

"And she wants you to bring me some Mary Kay samples from the closet at the end of the hall."

Whatever. "Sure."

Kendra looks at me. "You impersonated a rhino keeper at the front desk so I'd come down. And you did this to see if you could ride with me to the Wild Animal Park? Are you always this resourceful?"

I think about my low grades at school and my lack of success in beginner swimming. "No."

Then I think about all the research I did on Josh, finding out his classes, what sports he does and who he dated. "Sometimes."

Finally I think about my mother and wanting to save her afterlife by solving the mystery. "When it counts."

Kendra smiles. "Be here by nine o'clock." She calls out to the front desk, "Mr. Lopez." She winks at me. "Sue will be meeting me again tomorrow morning." Then she goes all serious. "Don't be late."

I watch the elevator doors close and the floor numbers light up. With each rising number, my spirits climb. I am so handling this mystery. And I'm going to be resourceful—love that word—one more time tonight. I walk to the reservations desk.

"Mr. Lopez?" I ask.

He comes over to me straightaway. "Yes, Sue."

"Do you have any copies of the *Union-Tribune*?"

"Certainly." He pulls out a perfectly folded newspaper from under the counter. He slides it toward me. "Do you need anything else? The *New York Times*? *LA Times*? *London Times*?"

Times, Times, Times. Sounds like someone got a little lazy when coming up with a name for their newspaper. "I wouldn't mind a couple of those free-ice-cream vouchers."

I think I catch a hint of a grin on his face as he hands me a bunch of coupons. "Take extra." He pushes up a shirt cuff and glances at his watch. "The café is open for another thirty minutes."

"Thanks, Mr. L. Do you happen to know if they have sprinkles?"

"You're welcome, uh, Sue. And, yes, I believe so." He's definitely grinning.

I pocket the coupons and pull out my cell. I know exactly who to invite.

✕   ✕   ✕

Seated next to the outdoor heater at the Hotel Del Café, I'm basking in the furnace blast of warmth. I dig into a huge double-coupon bowl of chocolate ice cream with walnuts and hurts-your-teeth fudge sauce.

Across from me, Junie spoons up vanilla smothered in rainbow sprinkles. The two of us have been serious ice cream addicts forever. I bet we've eaten the equivalent of a small planet over the years.

"Guess who's coming to San Diego?" I say.

Junie shrugs.

"Josh Morton. On Thursday. And we're getting together."

"Sherry!" Junie stops eating mid bite. This says a lot about Junie's level of excitement for me. "That's fantastic. What are you going to wear?"

"My good-luck outfit."

Junie nods.

I unfold the newspaper.

"*You're* reading the newspaper?" Junie asks.

I raise my hands in mock horror. "Absolutely not." I push a couple of sections of the paper toward her side of the table. "Don't you kinda think Rob's a poseur?"

She doesn't hesitate. "No."

That's the thing about Junie. She pulls off beyond-awesome grades at school. I swear she knows more than most of our teachers. But when it comes to reading people, she sucks. I say, "I wonder how many articles Rob wrote in this issue."

Junie unfolds a section. "Why?"

"Just to know."

"You're on." She starts reading. Junie and knowledge go together.

"You don't need to actually read the articles," I say. "Just glance to see who wrote them."

"You mean look for the byline?"

"Uh, yeah. The byline."

There's silence except for the crinkling of newspaper. More noise comes from my side of the table because I'm turning pages faster than Junie. I think I may have a scanning talent.

"Here's an interesting article." Junie looks up.

"Is it by Rob?"

"No, but it's about Damon Walker and *Murder on the Beach*. Apparently, he's had trouble getting financial backing, but he believes in the movie so much, he's bankrolling a lot of it himself."

My mind whirs like a ceiling fan in the Phoenix summer. Damon was very down on the rhinos. Any chance he's running out of money? I wonder how much a rhino horn goes for. I'll quiz Kendra tomorrow about her boyfriend and money.

I scoop up a spoonful of ice cream. "No Rob Moore bylines. You find any?"

"None for me either," she says. "So?"

"So? Rob totally lied about being a big-time reporter." I pull the used Wild Animal Park ticket out of my mini-backpack and push it toward her. "And he totally lied about not going to the Park. This ticket fell out of his pocket. And he tried to talk us out of going there."

"So?"

"So, don't you think it's all just a little suspicious? Like maybe there really is a mystery at the Park? And Rob's investigating it? Or maybe he's even guilty of something?"

"Yeah, I think Rob's guilty of something," Junie says. "Guilty of trying to impress Amber."

Hmmmm. Maybe. And maybe of something even more devious.

chapter 20

It's nine a.m. Monday morning, my first full day in San Diego. Kendra and I are in her rental Jeep Wrangler, zooming north. The wind is whistling and whipping in through the half doors, attacking the many plastic grocery bags on the backseat. Because I wasn't sure which Mary Kay products Kendra would use, I grabbed a few of everything.

Junie and Amber left crazy early for their big debut as extras. I told them I was going to the Wild Animal Park with a tour group from the Hotel Del. I didn't want to lie, but I was worried Amber would spill the beans to Damon about Kendra going to the Park. Besides, Junie's made it clear she doesn't want to hear anything even remotely mystery related. Because she's so convinced there isn't a mystery.

I'm cutely outfitted for detecting in navy shorty shorts and a white blouse with teeny cornflowers around an elastic scoop neck. I'm carrying a large, floppy denim hat. Sadly, Kendra's dressed only slightly better than last night. She's wearing old-lady clothes: a tan safari-shorts-and-button-down combo with a thick masculine belt. She'd definitely earn a Fashion Ewwww.

Both sides of the highway are blanketed with blindingly bright red, orange and yellow plants. Miles off in the distance, green hills are dotted with rocks that look like huge Pippi Longstocking freckles. It's like I'm in a high-def Nickelodeon cartoon.

"Sherry," Kendra asks, "how'd you know about the unauthorized rhino treats?"

I won't answer. I can't tell her about my mom because of Academy rules. Plus, I don't want to. I don't need even more people thinking I'm whacked. Cupping my ear, I say, "Huh? Huh? Can't hear you."

She raises her voice. "How'd you know about the unauthorized rhino treats?"

After pasting on a puzzled look, I mouth, *Can't hear you*.

Jaws open wide like a whale's, Kendra screams each word individually. "How. Did. You. Know. About. The. Rhino. Treats!"

Help. She'll never give up. After drawing an X across my chest with my index finger, I answer in a normal voice, "I promised I wouldn't tell."

She picks up her sports bottle and squirts water down her throat. Then she slings a slit-eyed look at me.

"I can't break a promise, Kendra. Sorry—really—but I have my integrity to consider."

Before I can pop off a question about Damon's finances, she asks, "How'd you get so interested in helping the rhinos?"

Kendra, stop already. She's like Nancy Drew's obnoxious big sister. "My mother."

"Your mother?" Her eyes widen, even the smaller one. "Does she work with rhinos?"

"Not that I know of. She's just, uh, you know, interested in them."

There's only the sound of the wind zipping around the Jeep, rattling the plastic bags while Kendra digests this.

I get straight to the point. "So, I read in the paper that Damon's having a hard time getting money for his movie. Is it true?"

Kendra brushes me off like I'm a nerdy thirteen-year-old. "Want to hear the speech I'm giving at the ceremony?"

Eventually we exit the highway and drive along a two-lane road. We pass wooden fruit-and-vegetable stands and signs for an ostrich farm. The closer we get to the Park, the more all-business Kendra gets. She practices parts of her speech out loud. I learn that rhino horns are worth a lot on the black market. People buy them for dagger horns and quack medicines. Kendra's emotional and angry when she says this part.

She's very single-minded when it comes to the rhinos. Seems like Damon's very single-minded about his movie. Too bad they aren't single-minded about the same thing.

We turn up the drive to the Park, and Kendra pulls into a spot in the parking lot. Then we hurry up the hill to the entrance, where she flashes her ID and I hand over one of the free passes. Next we hustle along until we reach what looks like a small

African village with a little picnic area and a bunch of grass-roofed buildings. By the wooden signs I can tell they're restaurants and gift shops.

"This is Nairobi Village, where the ceremony will be. I better check in." Kendra glances around. "Let's get you settled in a front-row seat."

I don't think staying for the ceremony is a good plan for me. No, I definitely need to poke around the Park. And buy a coffee to call my mother with. "I'm going to look around first."

"Well, okay, but don't take too long, or you'll miss the beginning of the ceremony," Kendra says. "I'll be done in a couple of hours. Do you need a ride back to Coronado?"

"Definitely."

She flips her wrist to see her watch. "See you after the speech. Let's meet at the picnic area." And she takes off.

I wait till she's out of sight before heading over to one of the little hut places for coffee. When I get to the front of the line, I ask, "What's your largest size?"

The woman, decked out in the same unattractive safari outfit as Kendra, holds up a Styrofoam cup.

I frown. I mean, we're many miles away from downtown San Diego. I don't see how my mother could find me from that cup. "Nothing bigger?"

Safari Waitress frowns. "It's a large. Twenty ounces."

I look at the stuff displayed around her window. "How about the bucket for the kid's meal?"

"You want me to fill the children's meal container with coffee?" From her tone, you'd think I asked her to spend the night in the

114

tiger exhibit. With hunks of raw steak as a pillow. "That's a lot of coffee."

I shrug. "That's how I roll."

She shakes her head like it's all too bizarre. "I don't have a lid that'll fit."

"No problem. I'm extremely coordinated." I smile wide. "And could ya make it strong? No milk or whipped cream or sugar."

Across her little ledge, Safari Waitress passes me the bucket of coffee, still shaking her head. "Be careful. It's hot."

"Which way are the rhinos?" I grip the flimsy handle with both hands.

"The rhino exhibit's quite a walk from here. You'd be better off taking the monorail." She frowns. "After you finish your coffee. No drinks allowed on the train."

"Okay." I'm all noncommittal.

Clutching the bucket to my stomach and trying not to slosh, I lurch in the direction she indicated. This sucker is heavy. I hope my mom shows up soon. Before my arms fall off.

Suddenly, bobbing in the middle of the crowd up ahead, I spy a familiar head of orange orangutan hair.

The familiar head of Monkey Man!

chapter 21

It's detecting time. An eye on Monkey Man, I cram on my floppy hat and grasp tight with numb fingers to the bucket of coffee.

I fight my way through the people until only a few families separate us. Not easy while juggling a gazillion gallons of steaming caffeine. When Monkey Man joins the monorail line, I drop back and hide behind a wooden column. The sec he's seated and looking away from me, I shuffle toward the train.

"No food or drink on the monorail," a girl in a safari outfit says. The Park obviously got a huge discount on ugly uniforms. She waggles a finger toward a waste bin.

I switch directions, trying not to cause a tsunami in the bucket. When she's not looking, I hug the bucket in close and cover it with my hat. I'm so not dumping the coffee, aka my phone line.

Hunched over and chin tucked, I walk sideways to the end of the train. Safari Girl is boarding, her back to me. I speed up.

Slosh. Slosh. Slosh.

Hot. Hot. Hot.

Ouch. Ouch. Ouch.

Ack. A huge, ugly coffee stain spreads across my previously adorable white blouse. Not even industrial-strength stain remover is gonna help this disaster.

I snag a spot alone in the caboose compartment a couple of rows behind Monkey Man. I set the bucket on the floor and smooth out my shirt.

Monkey Man's sitting by himself too. His apishly long left arm hanging outside the car, he's tapping the metal side with his fingers and staring out at the bush.

In case he looks back, I slump down in the seat, tugging the brim of my hat low over my eyes. Then I get my bearings. There's a canopy roof above, and the sides of the train, open from about three feet up, give way to a panorama of the savanna. It's brown dirt, ponds with green water and patches of grass and shrubs. Very *National Geographic*.

Lots of families are on board. In front of Monkey Man, a frazzled mom jiggles a fussy baby on her lap while her toddler bugs the poor other woman in the compartment.

At the front of the train, Safari Girl stands. "Good morning, folks. My name is Hannah. And I'm going to take you on an exciting safari through the wilds of Africa."

117

With a jerk, we're off.

Hannah drones on and on about our surroundings and the animals and their habits. She inches the train forward, stops, talks and inches forward again.

My phone starts to ring. Ack. I slap it off quickly. It's a text from Junie. I text her back, and we get a conversation going. Which is good, because I'm seriously tired of animal trivia.

> **Junie:** im so bored at this movie
> shoot.
> **Sherry:** ur kidding
> **Junie:** all i do is sit and fake—
> read a bk on the beach. Amber gets
> 2 walk arnd in a bikini. Shes
> flirting with every guy & ignoring
> me. Wut r u doing?
> **Sherry:** im on the monorail at the
> park. Super exciting. Ud <3 it.
> **Junie:** really?
> **Sherry:** yeah. Its gr8.
> **Junie:** can I meet you there? We're
> almost done. Amber can drop me off.
> **Sherry:** Meet me at entrance. Like
> in 2 hrs. I'll ride back with u
> guys.

Yay. Junie's coming to the Wild Animal Park. Everything is better when you're with a friend.

Monkey Man sneezes.

"The acacia trees are in bloom," Hannah says. "Sounds like we have an allergy sufferer on board."

I do a mental high five. With his sneezing, I'll never lose him.

"Folks, look under the palm tree on the left side of the train." Hannah points. "See the group of female rhinos? The females are very sociable and like to hang out together in a group called a crash."

Hannah, puhleeze, put the pedal to the metal. I only have two hours till Kendra's speech ends. I gotta figure out what Monkey Man is up to.

"Look over by the water hole. It's Frank, our Cape buffalo. An extremely aggressive animal." She slows the train. "In fact, Fightin' Frank is being moved to his own enclosure later today because he's been bullying the other animals."

"What's the hut for?" a woman calls out.

I glance at the small stucco building.

"That's the rhino keeper's," Hannah answers. "The white rhino lying in the shade by the door is Ongava." She stops the train. "He's our youngest male calf. Until Gina's calf arrives, that is."

"What's the calf doing by the hut?" the same woman asks.

"He probably wants to be near Sue, our head rhino keeper." Hannah continues, "Rhinos have a terrific sense of smell, and Ongava loves Sue's shampoo, Sassy Girl."

Just like mine.

"In fact, all our rhinos love it. Sue keeps a few bottles in the hut. Then, when she wants the rhinos to change location, she dribbles Sassy Girl on the ground. They just follow the shampoo trail."

Obviously, Hannah could talk for centuries about animals. I drift off into my fave daydream. The one where Josh and I are slow-dancing at a school dance. I'm snuggled up against him. He's moving in for a kiss.

A child screams from way up front.

I sit up straight and look around. A giraffe is loping toward the first compartment.

The kid screams again.

"I made it," a familiar voice says beside me.

I scream. My palm pressing down on my chest, I whisper, "Mom, you almost gave me a heart attack."

"I'm impressed I actually managed to find this place. And I successfully negotiated a monorail landing. That's two firsts for me today." She's probably patting herself on the back. "The bucket of coffee was very helpful."

"Thank you, thank you." I mock-bow from the waist, then point to Monkey Man. "See that guy with the long arms? He's the one from the tennis courts. Who dropped all the weird seed." I look around. "Where's Grandpa?"

"Your signal was so strong; I told him he could stop in the aviary for a bite to eat."

Another scream from the front of the train.

"What's going on up there, anyway?" I crane my neck for a clearer view.

A giraffe's head bobs closer and closer to a little girl. His tongue, long and skinny, wriggles through the air toward a green, leaflike barrette in the kid's hair.

"Don't worry, folks." Hannah stands. "He can't get any nearer. What a great close-up view of a giraffe's blue-black tongue."

"Gross." I make a face. "That tongue looks like it was in a fight. And lost."

"Sherry, Sherry," my mother whispers, all agitated. "He jumped down."

I peer over the side of the monorail. Ack. Eek. Awk. Monkey Man's hoofing it across the plain.

"Jump. Sherry, now. While everyone's staring at the giraffe."

I look over the edge again. And waaaay down. Too far. "No, I'll break my legs."

"Sherry, you can do it."

Can you believe my *mother* is asking me to do this? "There are wild animals down there. With teeth. And claws."

"I'll be with you. I told you how well I did in my Animal Mind Control class. I'll plant thought suggestions to keep the animals away from you."

"Like 'Eat the clump of grass, not the tasty girl'?" Right. This from the woman who can only find me in the presence of coffee. The woman who crash-lands everywhere. The woman who floats off in the middle of a conversation. I squeeze as far into the corner as possible. "Nuh-uh."

My cell phone rings. I look at the screen. Josh! "Mom, I'll do the detective thing when we're back at the monorail station. Promise."

"You're letting a hot trail grow cold."

"I'm not jumping. I don't want to die," I say, flipping open the phone. "I'm taking this call."

"Hey, Sherry," Josh says.

That voice, that voice, that voice. I would follow it anywhere. I'm goose bumped from head to toe, inside and out.

"There's a change—" he says.

My cell is rudely ripped from my hand and tossed over the side of the train. Josh's golden tones grow fainter and fainter. "Sherry? Sherry? Are you—" His voice cuts out.

I watch in horror as the phone spirals down, whirling and twirling, glinting and gleaming in the air. It splats on the dirt.

Hannah cries, "Here comes another giraffe."

And my right leg is up and over the side of the monorail before you can say "You'll pay for this, Mom." I hang on for a second with curled fingers, then belly-flop onto the hard-as-cement ground. My hat sails off my head and lands at the top of a small, prickly tree.

My breath whooshes out. I lie still, flattened, corpselike, full of pain.

chapter 22

Finally, finally, my squashed lungs manage to suck in some air. Just in time too. My head's spinning and starry from lack of oxygen. I lick my lips. Ewwww. Spit. Spit. Spit. My mouth is caked with dirt.

I feel a flutter.

"Sherry, pumpkin, are you okay?"

I wheeze, "Maybe."

Then I stretch out ultracarefully on the scorching-hot ground. No broken bones. Raising my head on my nearly snapped neck, I watch the train move away. A few feet in front of me, my phone sparkles in the sunlight. I commando-crawl over, grab it and stick it to my ear. No sound. I blink at it. No screen graphics. I push the On button. Nothing. My phone is completely and totally defunct.

"Sherry, pumpkin, talk to me."

I pull myself up to my feet and brush off. "Go away." I cross my arms and stick my nose in the air. "I am so not speaking to you."

"Sherry—"

I slide my finger and thumb across my closed lips like I'm zipping them, then throw away the pretend key.

My mother sighs.

An animal bellows long and low and mean.

The hairs on my arms stand straight up like toothpicks. I spin around to see a huge black animal squinting in the glaring sun at me. He has drooping, fringed ears and wide, curved horns. And he stinks like a barn.

Holy cow. It's the superaggressive Cape buffalo. Only thirty feet away.

"Mom?" I squeak. "Mind thoughts?"

"On it. I'm directing its focus to a tree across the savanna."

The buffalo's small, dark eyes slit. He snorts. A line of snot dangles from his nose.

"I have never met a more stubborn animal. His brain is really locked up." Mom's voice is low and forced, like she's trying to pick up something heavy.

The creature paws the ground with a hoofed foot.

"Help, Mom."

"Let me try a different method."

There's silence while she's doing I-don't-know-what.

"Sherry"—her pitch jumps up—"nothing's working."

Blood pounds in my ears.

Then she's right by me. "Run to the hut. I'll distract him."

I want to run. I do. Run fast. But I can't move. It's my same-o lame-o problem. Faced with a scary situation, I freeze.

"Mom, Mom, Mom." The words come out hoarse and strangled.

"Sherry, you can do this." She sounds supershaky.

Flies land on the buffalo's head and crawl toward his nostrils. He shakes his head, rippling the muscles along his massive shoulders. His horns glint in the sun. His half-shut eyes never leave me.

A tree drops a long, lavender blossom onto my shoulder. I don't brush it off. I can't even budge my arms.

The buffalo snorts again.

"Run!" Mom screams.

I'm rigid. Like wood. Sweat trickles down my back. A strand of hair blows into my eye. The sizzling ground burns through the soles of my shoes.

And then suddenly I can move.

It's exactly like someone flipped a switch, releasing me from frozenness. Like it's spring in Narnia. I lift one foot, jut my elbows back, ready to dash fast like a bullet.

"Go, Sherry."

Then slowly and gently, I plant my foot back down.

"Go! Go!"

I straighten my arms out up by my shoulders like branches.

"Run, Sherry! Run!"

"No," I whisper out of the side of my mouth.

In my mind, I see a particular paper cup from the bathroom at home. In lime-colored letters, it details the story of a safari guy who acted like a tree in the middle of a buffalo stampede. And lived to tell his tale. And have it printed on a paper cup.

"Sherry! Run! Right this minute!"

I imagine bark on my legs and leaves growing out of my head.

There's rustling to the right of me. Out of the corner of my eye, I see Ongava, the rhino calf, grazing. Chewing, he looks up at me. He steps toward me.

Oh great. He's probably attracted to my hair, washed this morning with Sassy Girl.

Ongava takes another step in my direction.

Yikes. Is it my destiny to be the cream in an Oreo cookie of smelly zoo animals? No, no, no. No bad thoughts. I'm a great tree. I can do this. I can do this.

My mom's yelling at me. She sounds all slow-motion and muffled, like she's under water. I'm trapped in my own little time warp.

Hopefully those Dixie-cup people check their facts.

The buffalo paws the ground, scattering dust.

The calf trots right up to me.

I glimpse a grayish blur stirring under the palm tree and heading toward our little group. It's the female crash.

My life flashes before my eyes, a bunch of things I wish I'd done differently. I could've been nicer to Sam. I could've been nicer to The Ruler. I could've been less of a drag for Junie. I could've grabbed Josh in the nurse's office and kissed him. I don't want to die a squishy-stinky animal death.

The crash approaches. They stop and face the buffalo, then

grunt. The buffalo stares at the female rhinos. Then he stares at me.

A breeze comes up, carrying a sweet flowery smell. A crow caws in the distance. The sun blazes down hot on us.

We're in it together. It's me and the rhinos against the buffalo.

The calf snorts. The female rhinos grunt again. I hold my breath in a treelike way. The buffalo paws the dirt one last time before turning and tramping away.

The rhinos call to Ongava, then saunter back to the shade. The calf follows them. I let out my breath.

"Sherry, thank goodness you're okay." Mom blows my sweaty bangs off my forehead.

I watch the rhinos' cute little tassely tails swing as they amble away. Their adorable leathery skin gleams in the sun. I think fondly of their kind, squinty eyes.

I'm alive. We're all alive—me, the female crash and Ongava. Today I shared a near-death experience with the big, beautiful rhinos. We're forever connected. Cross my heart, I promise to find out who's trying to hurt you. I'll hunt him down and stop him. No more fooling around. You are my soul mates, and you can count on me. I will face challenges head-on and succeed. From this point forward, I am Sherlock Holmes Baldwin, Fearless Rhino Warrior.

"Let's get out of here," Mom says.

"Not speaking to you."

"Sherry, I'm so sorry. I wouldn't purposely put you in danger."

"You threw my phone and my love life off the monorail."

The door to the hut opens. A girl in an ugly tan safari uniform leans out. "Get in here before you get yourself killed," she orders.

On Jell-O legs, I wobble my way toward the hut. And away from my mother.

"Are you crazy?" The girl clutches my arm and yanks me through the door.

Californians are so rude. Suddenly, the room is spinning.

"Hey, are you going to faint?" She eases me into a chair, then gets me a wet paper towel. "Who are you?"

I press the paper towel against my forehead and close my eyes. "Sherry Baldwin."

"I'm Sue, the rhino keeper. This is my boyfriend, Thomas."

I open my eyes and gasp.

There, sitting across the tiny room with his arms practically scraping the floor, is Monkey Man.

chapter 23

Sue would definitely be grounded if she lived at my house. The rhino hut's a disaster, junked up with things like tie wraps, duct tape, bottles of Sassy Girl shampoo, trash from McDonald's. The place reeks of old fries and dirt and animals.

I look over at Monkey Man. The rhino keeper's boyfriend. Mind-boggling.

He looks down, but not before a flash of recognition flits across his face. He remembers me from the tennis courts.

"You're very lucky you didn't try to run," Sue says. "The buffalo feels less threatened by someone standing completely still."

"You will not believe where I learned that technique. These bathroom cups—"

Hands on hips, she interrupts, "Is there a reason you jumped down from the monorail?"

"I dropped my cell phone."

Her eyes go jumbo round like doughnuts.

"It's brand-new."

"You entered a wild-animal enclosure because of a cell phone?" Sue says. "That's incredibly irresponsible."

"Plus, I was talking to a dreamy guy." And I suddenly remember I have no idea what Josh called about.

"Do you even realize what a huge risk you took?" Her voice quakes with anger.

"Obviously not, or I wouldn't have dived for my phone." I shrug. "I'm not a complete moron."

She gawks at me. "Let's get you over to the Park office."

My stomach churns like a blender on low. "The Park office?"

"They'll get some information from you, then someone will escort you off the grounds."

The blender kicks up to medium. "Why?"

"You're a danger to yourself and the animals," Sue says. "We can't have you here."

Now the blender is blasting away at full power, chopping and grinding. If I'm banished from the Park, how am I supposed to fulfill my destiny as a Fearless Rhino Warrior and save the rhinos?

Wait just a sec, Sue. The stomach blender slows as I realize I have some ammo.

"I'm not the only one who jumped off the monorail," I say.

Sue and Thomas exchange a look.

"That's different. He's a, uh, trained professional," Sue says in a way-less-mean voice.

My Fearless Rhino Warrior side hooks up with my detective side to tell me something's not right. "So Monkey—I mean, Thomas—works here?"

"Well, not exactly." Sue draws out the words.

What exactly does "not exactly" mean? I decide to try the intimidating-cop routine that's so successful on TV shows.

I cross my arms and lean toward her. I furrow my forehead, aiming for the frightening-unibrow look. "Where does he work?"

"At the ostrich farm down the road."

"And how does that make it okay for him to jump down from the monorail?" I ask, all low and bad-cop husky.

"He totally connects with animals, which means he's not in danger and they're not in danger," Sue says. "They trust him."

Trust him enough to eat seedy-pellety poison from him? "So he's like Dr. Dolittle?"

"He can tell if they're sick or pregnant or depressed." Her eyes flash. "And Thomas *should* be working here. His talents are wasted at the ostrich farm."

"Why isn't he, then?"

"He will be. He's trying," Sue sputters.

I can't really think of how poisoning the rhinos could help Thomas get a job here, but maybe I'm missing something. Or maybe he's so peeved at not getting a job that he's taking it out on the rhinos.

Thomas clears his throat and taps his watch. "Lunchtime."

I almost fall off my chair. He speaks. What a shocker. I was

131

starting to believe he couldn't because he was, like, mute or French or something.

Sue takes a deep breath. "Look, Sherry . . ."

"Sue, I will never jump off the monorail again, and I won't rat Thomas out." I cross my fingers behind my back because I'll do whatever it takes to bust him if he's the guy after the rhinos.

She nods.

He nods.

I nod.

It's like we all have Slinky necks.

"Let's get you off the savanna," Sue says.

The three of us leave the hut and head to a tan pickup parked nearby. Sue scoots in behind the steering wheel. I take the passenger seat. Arms swinging, Thomas climbs into the bed.

"I'm going to drop you at the entrance," Sue says. "Thomas and I only have an hour for lunch."

A devious plot hatches in my detective brain.

chapter 24

The nanosecond the pickup pulls out of view, I'm off. I run out of the Park, down the drive, along the soft shoulder until I reach a small white sign. SAN DIEGO RATITE FARM. Ratite? I guess that means "ostrich." I take a left and huff and puff to the end of a short, potholed dirt driveway. Another small white sign hangs from a wire fence. ENTRANCE TO THE SAN DIEGO RATITE FARM BY APPOINTMENT ONLY.

Is nothing easy in mystery solving?

Gripping my knees, I lean over, trying to catch my raggedy breath. I can feel blisters bumping up between my toes. Why did I wear sandals?

I hear shuffling and look. Eeks. Ikes. It's a huge ostrich. With flat red feet and ugly, bony legs. Cocking its head, it fixes me with sad eyes.

I gaze behind it, down a hill to where a gazillion ostriches stand or walk around. A few sit on the dirt ground. On eggs, maybe. Poor things. No trees and a blazingly hot sun.

I look back up at the ostrich by the fence. "Hey, boy. How ya doing?" I cluck at him.

The big bird tilts his head to the other side, his eyes on me. He lifts one long, flat foot, sets it down with a thump and then lifts the other foot. He shakes his brown tail feathers and bobs his head from side to side.

Is he asking me to dance? I raise my right foot, then my left, and step heavily into the dirt to mimic the thumping sounds of the ostrich's big feet.

"I see Kevin Bacon's got you dancing," a gravelly voice says.

On the other side of the locked gate stands a Weeble-like old man scratching his sticky-out belly.

"Kevin Bacon?" I search my memory. I think he was a teenage dancer in an old movie.

"Are you the egger I been expectin'?" The man hooks his thumb in a belt loop. "You're half an hour late."

"Egger?"

"Someone who decorates eggs," he says. "So, if you're not the egger, what're ya doin' here?"

Um. Um. "I'm doing a report for school on ostriches."

He points a long, dirty nail at the sign. "Go home and phone for an appointment."

"I'm all the way from Arizona. Couldn't you spare a few

134

minutes?" I smile sweetly. "I won't take long." Seriously. The clock is ticking as I speak. Between Kendra and her rhino ceremony and Thomas and his lunch break, I don't have much time.

The farmer picks a long stem of grass and sticks it between his teeth, chewing on it for a while. "Okay," he finally says. "But you're out of here when the egger shows up. I don't do double appointments."

"Thank you so much."

Kevin Bacon plods off to join his feathered friends, abandoning me to the grumpy old guy.

The farmer reaches into his jeans pocket and pulls out a rusty key. He unlocks the gate and lets me in. He gestures with his head. "You can see the birds better from over this way." He ambles along, slow like a slug.

I speed up in the hopes he'll match my pace. Uh. No. Apparently not. I slow back down.

"So, what do ya wanna know?"

My questions are all about Thomas, but I'll have to slide those into the conversation. "I didn't realize ostriches were so big."

" 'Cuz of me, our birds are extra healthy," he brags. "They have more meat, hide and feathers than at other farms. And restaurants love our tender meat."

Meat? Hide? Feathers? "What? You kill the ostriches?"

He looks at me like I'm a drooling idiot. "Did you think this was the Wild Animal Park?"

Honestly, I've spent as much time contemplating ostrich farms as I have speaking Chinese. I certainly didn't know people ate ostriches. Well, yuck.

I'm walking along, pretty grossed out, when I realize something grainy is underfoot. I look down. It's the same weird seedy-pellety mixture I found on the tennis courts!

I bend over and let some dribble through my fingers. Definitely the same stuff. "What's this?"

The farmer scowls. "Our own feed."

"Feed? Not poison?"

He snorts. "Definitely not poison."

"What's in it?"

"How would I know?" He spits at the ground. "It was developed by a jerk who works here. Only he and the owner know the secret recipe."

"Is the jerk named Thomas?"

"How did you know?"

"Um, um, I phoned here once."

"I'm surprised he picked up. He usually just lets it ring. He's not much of a talker."

"Yeah, he does seem pretty weird." Look at me, getting info out of this guy.

"You don't know the half of it." The farmer plucks his straw hat off his head and runs his fingers through thinning, greasy hair. "Thomas's main friends are the birds. I've seen them get up off their eggs for him. Almost like they're giving him a gift."

"How else do you get the eggs?"

"I go in with the dogs. The birds can get real aggressive." He hitches up his jeans by the waistband. "The dogs are always willing to help me out 'cuz I treat them to a little raw ostrich meat mixed in with their dog food."

Ugh. Disgusting visual. "Why don't you leave the eggs with the ostriches?"

"They hatch better in an incubator."

My mind's grasshoppering all over the place. If Thomas is whipping up batches of healthy feed and is trusted by ostriches, he's probably exactly how Sue described him: an animal lover. Not an animal hater. Not a rhino killer. Although, why was he spying from the tennis courts?

Whatever. We're down to Damon, who needs money, and Rob, who needs a story. Or it could be someone I don't even know about. Ack.

"What else do ya wanna know?"

"Nothing," I say. Time to vamoose. I step in the direction of the front gate.

"That's enough information for a whole report?"

"I'm only aiming for a C." I take another couple of steps.

Finally, he starts his ambling thing. After about a million years, we reach the entrance. Straw between his teeth again, the farmer jiggles the key in the lock, then creaks open the gate.

I explode outta there.

chapter

25

Junie's waiting at the Wild Animal Park entrance for me. "Where were you?"

"An ostrich farm. I was following a suspect, and he works there, and—"

"Sherry. Stop." Junie cuts me off. "Try this." She hands me a wrapped candy. "I got a bunch of saltwater taffy from the candy store underneath the Hotel Del."

I slowly chew on tacky maple walnut. I know the candy is Junie's unsubtle way of shutting down the mystery conversation. But I won't be shut down. When I get my teeth unstuck, I say, "You know, I've put up with some strange stuff from you. And I was way, way more understanding."

"Are you referring to when I joined the chess club? 'Cause that's a lot different than asking me to believe your mom's a ghost, your grandfather's a wren and the three of you are solving a mystery about rhinos." Junie crosses her arms. "Also, for the record, you were not all that understanding."

I thought it was going to be better having a friend here. Maybe not. "Where's Amber?"

"Shopping. The only way I got her to bring me was by telling her about the mall nearby." Junie sighs. "She actually air-kissed someone when we were leaving the set. She's driving me insane."

And things are instantly improved between Junie and me.

I look at my wrist, where there'd be a watch if I wore one. "Time to meet Kendra Phillips," I say, just tossing it out there like it's an everyday occurrence.

"What?"

"She's how I really got up here this morning. I just told you guys I was taking a tour." We start walking toward Nairobi Village. "Because I was worried Amber would open her big mouth to Damon about Kendra coming to the Wild Animal Park. Which, judging from the argument we overheard, he's hard-core against."

Junie shakes her head back and forth like she's a shaggy dog who's drying off after a bath. "Wait. I'm still back at 'Time to meet Kendra Phillips.' "

So I tell her about impersonating Sue and how I scored the ice cream coupons.

"What's she like?"

"Into rhinos."

It's not often Junie's speechless. And I think I see a hint of respect in her eyes. Probably because I was resourceful, not because I'm solving a mystery.

We hook up with Kendra at a grass + dirt picnic area right by Nairobi Village. Surprisingly, she decides to grab chili in sourdough bread bowls with us, even after I tell her I don't need a ride back to the Del anymore. She must truly be hungry.

Once we're seated at a round plastic table, Kendra says, "So, Junie, are you as interested in rhinos as Sherry?"

"I don't know." Junie fidgets with her napkin. She's definitely uncomfortable with the rhino convo.

"We'll make you into a rhino lover." Kendra's eyes sparkle. She says to me, "According to Sue, we've got some new rhino fans who hang out by the fence. They met on an arthritis Web site. Let's go say hi, and I'll extend an official spokesperson welcome."

"I'm not up for a hike to the rhino exhibit. Not with the three nasty blisters I have on my right foot," I say. Also, I'm avoiding Sue.

"Sherry, you need to connect with the rhinos on their level, ground level." With a plastic spoon, Kendra scrapes the last of the chili from her bread bowl. "Up close and personal."

Like I don't know up close and personal with the rhinos. Not that I can tell her about it.

Seriously, though, I'm done. My lungs practically collapsed after my superhero leap from the monorail. A buffalo almost gored me to death. I've covered miles in my sandals. I spent time with a creepy ostrich farmer. I'm not exactly getting along with my mom. Bottom line: I need a nap.

I swallow a mouthful of Coke and prepare to whine.

Squawk. Squawk.

I squint up at the bright sky.

It's a raggedy shadow. It's an elderly wren. It's my grandpa.

He plops to the ground by my feet and starts pecking at crumbs.

Good. We need to talk about my mother. But in private. "Doesn't ice cream sound good?" I push out a groan. "I'd get it if I wasn't dealing with blisters."

Kendra frowns. "Actually, I could use a tea." She pushes back her chair and stands. "Ice cream is at a different kiosk. So you're on your own for that."

I look at Junie with big cow eyes.

"Fine," she says. "But you pay."

The second Junie and Kendra are out of earshot, I lean over. "Grandpa, where's Mom?"

With his beak, he scratches out the shape of a house in the dirt.

"The Whaley House? She went back to the Whaley House?"

He bobs his little head up and down.

I am brilliant. I pinch off some of my bread bowl and toss it to him.

He croaks, *Blah, blah, bad, blah, blah.*

I say, "Bad? She feels bad?"

Now *I* feel bad. Hate that mother guilt thing. "Fine." I huff. "I'll go talk to her later." I wag my finger at him. "Did she even tell you what she did to my cell phone?"

"Sherry, you are such an animal person. You're talking to that bird, aren't you?" Grinning, Kendra tugs on the tea bag string, swishing it around in her cup.

Junie comes up right behind Kendra. From the stony look on her face, she must've heard Kendra's question.

Not answering, I say, "Thanks, Junie." I reach for my soft serve.

Kendra swings her purse over her shoulder. "Let's hit the trail, girls."

I stand and take a few weak, limpy steps, then pause to lick my cone for strength.

Grandpa hops up onto the table and sticks his head into my bread bowl. He wrestles with it till he's got it clasped in his beak, then half-hops, half-flies behind me.

"Looks like you picked up a new best friend." Kendra grins again, then strides off, her purse bumping her back.

Junie's face goes even more closed.

Kendra's like a drill sergeant and forces us to march at an unhealthily fast clip. Too bad she's not megafamous with fans mobbing her every few feet for autographs. Instead, she keeps us moving nonstop, which means I have constant weight on my blisters. There is much pain involved in detective work.

Finally, while I still have a little feeling left in my feet, we arrive at the exhibit. Totally beat, I flop down on the grass and yank off my right sandal. Just as I suspected, one blister has ballooned to the size of a radish. The other two aren't much smaller.

Still dragging my bread, Grandpa bounces up next to me.

Junie stands across the path. Her eyes jump from Grandpa to me to Grandpa to me, over and over again. Like when a computer gets stuck and keeps looping through the same stuff.

I check out the fence. Sure enough, there's a bunch of extremely old people. Some are even leaning on walkers or canes. Incredible how determined they are to see the rhinos.

A bald man hunches forward in his wheelchair, binoculars glued to his face. "These animals appear to be very healthy. The Park must take excellent care of them," he says.

Enter Kendra with a friendly smile and an outstretched hand. "The Park does take excellent care of its rhinos."

Looking confused, Bald Man slowly extends his arm.

A tall, wrinkly woman with lavender hair and a matching cane says, "Who are you?"

Kendra blasts into a whole public-relations spiel. All about how involved she is in preventing rhino extinction, the documentary she did at some preserve in Africa, her duties as the Park's official rhino spokesperson. Her pitch rises; her volume varies; her eyes twinkle. Her body language is screaming rhino love and commitment.

And when she's done . . . silence. Complete silence.

Bald Man retracted his arm somewhere between "extinction" and "documentary."

Kendra flushes and her shoulders go all stiff.

Awkward, I mouth across the way to Junie.

A male voice calls out, "Kendra!"

We all turn to see a young, übercute security guy jogging down the path toward us. He's like something out of a sports-car commercial with his wavy brown hair blowing back in the breeze. And he's neat and put together in a uniform with creases and badges.

I think I'm all of a sudden attracted to guys in uniforms. Maybe

143

I'll suggest to Josh that he check into a part-time security job at the mall when he turns sixteen.

"Senior-discount cards, folks." Mr. Security Guy waves small cards in the air.

He has a British accent! Even cuter.

He smiles sincerely in Kendra's direction. "It's great to see you."

"You too, Gary." She relaxes her shoulders.

Most of the old people hobble over to him.

"Ladies and gentlemen," Gary announces, "allow me to introduce Kendra Phillips, our rhino spokesperson."

The old people look around at each other, at the ground, at their discount cards. Then they go back to talking among themselves. One reminds another to take a pill. Pretty soon they're all staring at the savanna, where Ongava's wandered over near the fence and is pulling on a clump of grass.

Kendra flushes again.

"Don't take it personally." Gary lowers his voice. "Most of them are in constant pain from arthritis. It's probably close to medication time." He makes a sweeping gesture with his arm. "You've got to appreciate their fascination with the rhinos. They literally spend hours watching them."

"Amazing," Kendra says.

Personally, I think it's too strange. What normal old person spends their retirement studying rhinos at the Wild Animal Park? What happened to shuffleboard and bridge and time-shares?

One frail woman stops rubbing a man's humped-up shoulder to point at a female rhino who left the crash for a drink at the water trough. Whoohoo. Such excitement. Really, there's only one

144

logical explanation for these fanatical rhino fans: They're old and losing it a little. Or a lot.

Grandpa flies over by Tall Lavender Lady. He's always liked purple.

"Any news on Gina giving birth yet?" Kendra asks.

"Nothing. But you can ask Sue yourself," Gary says. "She's coming down this way soon."

Ack. Eek. My sandal in my hand, I totter over to them.

Junie follows me.

I clear my throat. "Kendra, I'd kinda like to get going. I don't want this blister to get infected."

I think she does a mini eye roll before introducing me and Junie to Gary.

"Glad to meet you." Gary smiles. "Any friends of Kendra's are friends of mine."

"I first met Gary in South Africa," Kendra says. "He worked at the Lapalala Reserve, keeping it safe from poachers." She beams at him. "And he's an expert with a dart gun. Once a year, he'd inject birth control from a helicopter into female elephants to help manage the elephant population." She ups the beam to halogen intensity. "Very tricky, and he was the best."

"I read an article about that," Junie says. She starts asking him questions about elephants.

Boring subject, but I find I'm basking in Gary's overall adorableness. His eyes are the exact color of Hershey's Kisses. His voice is warm and genuine and wraps around me like a soft blanket.

All animated about Africa, Junie leans toward Gary.

145

She's flirting! In her own little intellectual way. Junie's definitely going through big changes this trip. Stammering around Ben, flirting with Gary. What's next?

I break loose from Gary's spell to look for Grandpa, who isn't by Tall Lavender Lady anymore. I limp past the fence and the group of old people plastered to it. I wave to the female crash, way off in the exhibit. Where's Grandpa?

Tall Lavender Lady and one of the old men stand close together, apart from the others. The old man is small and wrinkled. He's wearing a straw gardening hat and a sweatshirt with ARTHUR'S LANDSCAPING screen printed on the back.

I can always spot a budding romance. Just a little talent I have. With the incredible height difference, they make a sweet, odd couple. He says something about "two-step." How cute. They're planning a country-western dancing date. So much more appropriate than rhino ogling.

With gnarled, swollen fingers, he reaches into his pants pocket and slowly draws out a rolled-up Ziploc bag. He holds it in the palm of his hand while Tall Lavender Lady unrolls it.

"So, this is Keflit," she says. "Arthur, it's beautiful."

Keflit? Never heard of it. I inch up to them.

Yowser. Turquoise + sea green crystals. The exact same shade as my bedroom walls. Keflit would be perfect in my aquarium. And Tall Lavender Lady is right: Keflit is beautiful. Like royal jewels, the crystals glitter and gleam and dance in the sunlight.

"Love that Keflit," I say, joining them. "I have to have some for my aquarium." I reach out to touch the plastic bag. "Where'd you get it?"

Their jaws hit the ground.

Obviously they aren't used to Arizona friendliness.

"Junie," I call, "come see this. It's too cool."

"Vera, Vera." With shaking hands, Arthur shoves the bag toward her.

She slots it into the outside pocket of her purse. "It's not for an aquarium."

"That's okay," I say. "I decorate with a lot of stuff that isn't specifically for aquariums. I'm very creative."

"It's for planting," Arthur says.

Gary and Junie arrive.

"Junie, you've got to see these crystals. Finally, something for my aquarium that totally matches my walls."

Tall Lavender Lady doesn't pull the Keflit out for Junie to see.

"So, you're into fish?" Gary takes my elbow. "I used to be too." With his other hand, he takes Junie's elbow and leads us away. We pass Kendra, at the fence trying to schmooze with the old people. A lost cause, if you ask me. We pass Grandpa too. Asleep in a tree, his head tucked under a tattered wing, he's got a little snore going.

"What fish do you have?" Gary asks, all attentive.

"Tell him about Cindy and Prince," Junie says. By association with me, she's an aquarium aficionada too.

I'm diving into the habits of my bala sharks when Gary's cell chirps.

"I must get this." He takes a few steps before flipping open his phone. He probably wants some privacy, but I'm so tuned in to his yummy accent and his soothing voice that I can't turn off my listening. Plus, I'm worried it might be Sue saying she's on her way, because then I'll have to scurry out of here on my one functioning foot.

"I'm not available to talk at the moment." Gary rubs his forehead.

There's a pause, then he says, irritated, "No, I speak English." He disconnects.

Walking toward us, he's still frowning from his phone conversation. Then, like he's going on stage, Gary turns on a perfect smile. That never reaches his eyes.

chapter 26

The ride back is all about Amber.

Despite the fact that I'm grimy, exhausted and coffee stained, she convinces me to go to the Hotel Del's outdoor pool with her. Why? To watch her try on the new outfits she just bought. Why? She wants to make sure she doesn't clash with the pool area. Why? She's an extra in a scene that's getting shot there.

Yes, it's ridiculous. All I can say is, Amber's very persuasive. Junie got sucked in too.

When we get to the Del, Amber skips up the carpeted stairs to the rooms, right past the REGISTERED GUESTS ONLY BEYOND THIS POINT sign. She's borrowing a pool key from a guy she met on the set.

Junie and me slump in chairs in the lobby. Amber's many bags slump beside us. The hugest chandelier in history glitters above, showering us with glints of silver light.

"Got any games on your phone?" Junie asks.

"Doesn't matter," I say. "My phone's broken."

"It's probably out of charge."

"No, it fell." Really far.

"Try popping out the battery," Junie says, "then putting it back in."

Okay. That just sounds lame. But I'm desperate.

It works! When I snap the battery back in and push On, the screen lights up. I've got power. I've got messages. I've got phone.

"Junie, you're amazing."

She smiles.

The first message is from my great-aunt Margaret. "Sherry, just checking on you. I want to treat you and your friends to a pizza picnic on the beach Friday. Call me."

The next message is from my dad. He's checking on me too. He already talked to Sam, who's doing fine at Grandma Baldwin's house. Oh yeah, and The Ruler bought a few Hawaiian shirts for me and Sam. Probably with hideous, scary flowers that scream fashion disaster. Next she'll be buying matching muumuus for me and her. Help.

The last message is from Josh. My heart hammers like one of the Park's exotic birds I saw beak-attacking a tree trunk.

"Hey, Sherry. I guess we got cut off. Anyway, I'm coming out Tuesday, as in tomorrow. Not Thursday. Can't wait to see you."

I sigh with happiness.

"What is it?" Junie asks.

"Josh's coming to San Diego early. Tomorrow instead of Thursday."

Her mouth is round like a Cheerio. No words come out.

It's like I'm a Lava lamp and those colored blobs that float all over are blobs of love bumping around inside me, lighting me up.

I could happily stay in my Lava-lamp world till Josh arrives, replaying his message, zoning out over his freckles and deep blue eyes and sagging jeans.

But Amber skips back down the stairs. With the pool key.

She skips through the lobby and outside. Junie and me tramp behind her, carrying her bags. Actually, Junie tramps. Despite my blisters, there's a bouncy spring to my step because I have Josh on the brain.

While Amber's off changing in the poolside cabana, Junie and me get comfortable on the chaise longues. It's both cool and weird to be lying by a pool with palm trees from the beach waving in the ocean breeze and the sound of the ocean crashing in the background. It's like being in two places at the same time. Very exotic.

A couple of girls are tanning a few chairs away, flopped onto their stomachs and baking.

A family with a baby digs in a diaper bag for a special swim diaper and waterproof sunscreen. They seem pretty unaware of our existence.

"Isn't this hot, girls?" Amber prances back and forth in front of us wearing a thin pink T-shirt and ultrashort, low-rise pink

shorts. She's accessorized with pink sandals, huge pink hoop earrings and enough pink bracelets to cover her arm from her wrist
to her elbow.

"So, what do ya think?" Amber asks.

Junie shrugs.

"Looks, uh, pink," I say.

"Duh." Amber clinks the bracelets. "It's for the party I'm throw-
ing at your aunt's."

"What?" I shriek. "No way you're having a party! No way, José!
You can just lose that ridiculous idea!"

The tanning girls and the family tune in to us.

"Too late." Amber curls her thumbs through the shorts belt
loops and juts out her chest. "I already told everybody it's
on Friday."

"What?" I shriek again.

"You're going to a beach party on Friday," Junie says calmly.

"I am?" Amber's eyes sparkle. "I love double-party days."

"You should move your party to the beach," Junie says.

"Great idea," Amber says. "I love big parties."

I hope my aunt does too.

The tanning girls and the family go back to ignoring us.

"Wait'll you see what's next." Amber bounces off and returns in
a camouflage bikini.

A bikini that doesn't camouflage much of anything, if you get
my drift. Still, she does look good. And she definitely knows how
to swing her hips.

"So, what do ya think?" Amber asks.

Junie shrugs.

"Looks fine," I say. Anything not involving a party at my aunt's condo looks fine to me.

Next, Amber models a short black-and-gray-striped jersey dress with spaghetti straps. Then comes a baby-doll shirt with tight plaid capris. Then a halter dress with lace and large sunflowers.

By the fifth ensemble, Junie falls asleep. I'm kinda nodding off myself.

Amber shakes Junie's shoulders. Violently. "Give me feedback! Like, 'This outfit looks better worn by the towel rack instead of by the shallow end.' Or 'Those colors clash with your skin.' Or 'You need a spray-on tan.' " She glares at us. "This is my career. My future."

"Amber, you're from Arizona," Junie says. "Remember? The Grand Canyon State?"

"Yeah," I chime in, "since when did you go all Southern Cal with Hollywood fever?"

And then the strangest thing happens. Amber leans in close. So close I can see every perfect pore on her perfect face. On minty breath, she whispers, "I have insider info. About the movie."

chapter 27

Shaking my head, I drag my blistered feet up the steps to the Whaley House.

Who knew Amber would willingly give me a ride? Who knew Armber would ever give me mystery information? I'm still in shock. Sure, it was by accident. She doesn't know I'm investigating Damon. But still. What irony. And . . . who knew I'd ever use a term from English class in real life?

Anyway, according to a stagehand guy Amber met, Damon's expecting a bunch of money to come through soon for his movie. When that happens, it'll be the green light for him to hire more people. And some of them will actually get to say a line. Amber's hoping to be upgraded from an extra to an extra with a speaking part.

Will Damon's funding arrive in the form of a rhino horn?

At the door, a man in a top hat and an old-fashioned suit interrupts my thoughts. He says, all low and spooky, "Welcome to the Whaley House, the most haunted house in the United States, according to the Travel Channel."

I don't need this atmosphere stuff. My stomach is already fluttering like I'm carbonated. I am so not comfortable entering a haunted zone. I am so not comfortable facing a heart-to-heart with my mom.

The man holds out a white-gloved hand. "Ticket, please."

Ticket? "Uh, I'm just meeting my, uh, mom."

"There are currently no human visitors in the house."

"Oh, uh, I guess I got here early," I say.

He points at the small building next door. "Tickets are available at the museum."

I limp over, take care of business, then limp back.

The instant he's got my ticket, the docent starts feeding me facts about the olden days, all in the same creepy voice as before. "This brick house was constructed in 1856 by Thomas Whaley, who originally came to California for the gold rush." He brushes imaginary flecks off his lapel.

I take advantage of the break in his monologue. "I really just want to go in and look around."

He pushes round gold-rimmed glasses, probably fake, up his nose. "My talk is part of the tour. I'm sure you want to hear about our ghostly residents."

Why do I have to get the enthusiastic docent?

"There's Yankee Jim Robinson, one of the men who was

hanged on the exact spot where the house is," he says. "Thomas Whaley himself, dressed in a frock coat like the one I'm wearing. Then there's . . ."

I hum under my breath, just loud enough to tune out all the scary spirit babble.

"And you never know, young lady, who you'll meet today." The docent opens his eyes wide so that the whites are huge and freaky.

Ack. He's jinxing me.

He tips his hat. "Take your time. I'm going to run across the street for a bite, but I'll be available for questions when you're done."

I turn to watch as he heads down the steps, then waits at the curb for a break in traffic. I take a long last look at the sights and sounds of normal civilization. People are strolling along the narrow sidewalk, passing displays of postcards and Mexican blankets. An employee sweeps dirt off the stoop in front of an Indian jewelry store. The door to a soap store swings open, and a girl exits, chewing on a churro.

I take a deep breath and a small step. I cross the threshold.

It's completely quiet, the air heavy and still. Then the smell of coffee swirls around my head.

"Mom?"

"This is a nice surprise," Mom says.

"Yeah, well, I figured we should talk."

"Let's go upstairs where it's more private," she says. "It won't be long before the next batch of tourists arrive."

I follow the scent of coffee past the parlor, with its small chairs and organ, to narrow stairs with a smooth, polished banister.

At the top, there's a tiny theater. About forty wooden chairs face the stage and a painted backdrop of a lake and some grass. A black-and-white poster advertises a play about Yankee Jim Robinson.

A door with an EMPLOYEES ONLY sign creaks open, and I'm blown inside.

In the semidarkness, I bump against a small table and a dresser. I find a rocking chair and flop into it. Now the coffee mingles with a musty, closed-up smell. Squinting, I see I'm in a teeny room that I'm guessing was the prop room.

Mom's voice comes from above the dresser. "Do you know where your grandfather is?"

"I left him napping at the Wild Animal Park." I squirm around, trying to get comfortable in the hard chair.

"It was a long trip for him." She pauses. "Look, about your phone—"

"It's fine," I interrupt. "Not even broken."

"Sherry, we need to work as a team."

"I know, Mom. I know."

There's a short, awkward silence, then it's gone, like we both shrugged it off and moved on. 'Cause we love each other. 'Cause we're in this together. 'Cause we can't afford to be mad at each other. But it still kinda bugs me that we didn't really talk about it.

"So," Mom says, "what did you discover at the Park?"

Trying not to leave out any details, I fill her in on Thomas and Damon and everything I've been up to since morphing into a Fearless Rhino Warrior. I feel like I'm in a squad room or something. Like a real professional going over clues with a colleague.

"Sooo . . . ," Mom says slowly.

And I can just imagine her twirling her hair around her index finger.

"I understand Damon needs money," she says, "but there are much simpler ways than selling rhino horns on the black market."

"That's true for your average dude. But because of Kendra, Damon knows tons about rhinos."

"And depending on what Rob is willing to do, he may end up with a story *and* jail time." She pauses. "I wonder if he's like us. He knows something's going down with the rhinos, and he's following the leads in the hopes of scoring a scoop."

"Yeah, maybe." I rub the back of my knee.

"Then again, the perp could be someone completely different, someone we don't know about."

"True." I scratch my thighs.

"That chair is made of real horsehair," Mom says. "Maybe you're allergic."

I hop up. The last thing I need is another rash.

"Let's keep an eye on them both. I agree with you about Thomas being an animal lover, not a potential rhino killer." Then Mom asks, "What about the old people? They sound odd."

"They're past odd." And I tell her about them hooking up on the Internet and all having arthritis. "They hang out at the Park, drooling over the rhinos. And they're a really tight group. Like, reminding each other when to take medicine."

"So you think they're odd but harmless?"

"Exactly. Plus, they're rude." I put my hands on my hips. "And unfriendly."

I'm about to tell her about the Keflit and the new color on my bedroom walls, when I give myself a mental slap. I will not babble. I will stay focused and on task. Like a real, professional detective.

Mom says, "Sherry, now let me tell you what I've found out."

When my mom says she's been investigating too, I can totally tell by her voice she's already deep into Intense Mode.

My heart sinks. I absolutely hate it when she's in Intense Mode. We've been having such a nice, getting-along, figuring-things-out-together detective conversation. But now she'll go all-out crazy intense. And the more intense she goes, the more nonintense I go. After years of practice, it's cemented into our relationship. Once, in third grade, to counteract my mom's intenseness over multiplication facts, I completely shut down and got zeros on my timed tests for weeks.

Anyway, I bet she's sitting across from me, leaning forward with her elbows jammed into her thighs and her chin cupped by her palms. Her eyes are probably narrow like a lizard's and fanatically focused on me.

"I interviewed all the ghosts at the Whaley House." Her vowels are shortened and snapped off, like she can't spit them out fast enough.

"Interviewed"? More like "interrogated." "And?"

"Several talked about a famous French chef. He's living, not a ghost. Chef L'Oeuf. Prepares an annual dinner. Very top secret. Very exotic. New location every year. Last March was lion in London. Leaked to the press after the fact. By someone's nanny." Mom's sentences are short and reportlike. "Chef L'Oeuf has a dedicated following. Eccentric rich people. From all over the globe."

"So?"

"The chef's current location? San Diego. More precisely—Coronado Island."

"So?"

"Rhino meat. Is it on this year's menu?"

My Fearless Rhino Warrior instincts kick in. "That's illegal!"

"Correct. But immaterial to the chef. He believes his hush-hush meal operation is above the law. It always has been. His guest list includes some high-ranking officials. Like royalty and presidents of countries."

I shake my head to out the image of one of my rhino buddies shish kebabbed between a mushroom and a pineapple. No, no, no. That can't happen. "What do we do?"

"Tomorrow. Tuesday. Three p.m. sharp. On the Bay restaurant. Chef L'Oeuf will unlock the doors. You. Undercover. Enter the restaurant with the other workers."

"What?" She's lost it. My mother has totally lost it. "Hello." I wave my hand to break her insane military trance. "Ya don't think someone'll notice I don't actually work there? That I'm only thirteen?"

"Chef L'Oeuf trains a few students each spring," she replies. "Use 'career unit at school' to explain your presence."

"Got any ideas on how I should fake the cooking part?" I say with sarcasm. "I mean, Chef L'Oeuf *might* ask me to do something trickier than nuke a Hot Pocket, Mom."

She sighs. "Sherry, I doubt he'll assign you anything complicated. The dinner is planned for Friday. Tomorrow is a practice run for sauces, salad dressings and desserts." Then, because I'm not the only sarcastic one in the family, she adds, "Surely you can handle stirring with a wooden spoon."

I roll my eyes.

She sighs again. "You're all we've got. I can't cross the threshold to the restaurant. We can't send your grandfather in. Will we wait outside the restaurant, be available for backup or ideas if you need us? Absolutely."

"Fine." I huff. "What am I looking for? Exactly?"

"Exactly? I don't know. Chat with the workers. Keep your ears open. Look around. Are there any papers, recipe books? See if you can find out if he plans to serve rhino meat."

Sounds like mission impossible.

"And talk to him in French," Mom adds. "Apparently, it fatigues him to speak English and he's always looking for a little French conversation."

"Excusez-moi," I screech. "I don't speak French."

"It's one of your classes."

"I have a C minus in French. Translation: I. Don't. Speak. French."

Mom tsks. "Sherry, you always underestimate yourself."

I hate it when she makes statements like that. Especially when she might be right. "That's so not true," I yell at the air above the dresser. "I just happen to be realistic about my limits. Not like some people I know. Some people think they can handle anything. Some people go to drug busts when they're sick. And end up getting killed." The more I say, the more I can't stop myself. All this anger that I didn't even realize I had is rushing out of my mouth like water over the Hoover Dam. "You never really knew me. Not really. You knew your partner a gazillion times better

161

than me. You knew Nero Whatever-His-Last-Name, your dog partner, a gazillion times better than me. And now? Now you don't
know me at all. Not at all." For emphasis, I hold up my thumb and
index finger squeezed together. "So don't tell me I'm underesti-
mating myself. I don't speak French. End of story." I pound the
wall next to me.

Silence. Punctuated by gulps. Gulps on both our parts.

I'm not sure about my mother, but I feel sick. With the back of
my hand, I wipe tears off my cheeks.

Mom sniffs. "Sherry—"

Knock, knock.

I feel the blood drain from my face.

"What's going on in there? This area isn't open to the public."
The door swings open.

It's the docent. "You're not allowed in here." He peers at me
over his fake-o glasses. "Are you okay? You look like you've seen
a ghost." He claps. "You have. You have seen a ghost. Was it
Yankee Jim Robinson or Mr. Whaley?"

"Neither." And, staring at the dresser, I say, "It was an extremely mean and bossy ghost. With dumb ideas."

chapter 28

I flounce down the stairs and out into the sunlight. I'm fuming at my mom. And fuming at myself too. I wanted to make up with her. But, oh no, now it's worse than ever. I have a huge, hollow, not-getting-along-with-mom feeling in the pit of my stomach. Again. At some point, we'll have to have a big, fatty, emotional talk. Arghhh.

And just when I'm wallowing in the major drama of it all, I spot something that is guaranteed to improve my spirits. The Old Town Ice Cream Shoppe. A double scoop won't fix my problems, but it won't hurt them either. And I could certainly use a treat.

Minutes later, I'm blister-hobbling down the avenue with a double scoop, bubble-gum and cheesecake, in a sugar cone. A few licks, and I'm entering a less-stressed space. A few more licks, and I'm ready to call Josh.

I plop down on a bench at the side of the road. See, I know my limits. There's no way I can walk, eat, balance my phone and talk to Josh Morton all at the same time. So under the shade of a tall palm, I fish my cell from my mini-backpack. And prepare for a chat with the boy.

He picks up in the middle of the first ring and sounds so happy to hear my voice, I practically melt. A puddle of me + bubble-gum ice cream + cheesecake ice cream, right there on a Southern California sidewalk.

Josh: You free tomorrow around noon?

Me: Definitely.

Josh: Wanna meet at Belmont Park? It's this little amusement park in Mission Bay, right by the ocean.

Me: Definitely.

I disconnect and lean back on the bench, sticking my legs straight out and crossing them at the ankles. The sun's starting to set, and a salty ocean breeze caresses my face as I pop the last of the cone in my mouth.

Tomorrow is Tuesday. Tuesday. As in Twosday. Josh and Sherry. Sherry and Josh. Tuesday. Twosday. The most romantic day of the week.

My heart beating loudly with love, I pick myself up off the bench and head for the condo.

I push open the front door to the sounds of the TV. Walking down the pink hall, I identify the show. The evening news. Must be Junie watching it.

"Hi, Junie," I say.

From the pink couch, she jumps up, all startled. Junie doesn't just watch the news; she zones out on the news.

I ask, "Where's Amber?"

She sits back down, glues her eyes to the screen and doesn't answer till the anchorpeople break for commercials.

"She met a guy. She's on a date."

"What happened to Rob?"

"His boss sent him out of town to cover a car show."

"A car show?"

"Yeah. He'll be gone for a week. Turns out we were on to something when we couldn't find his byline. He's a pretty junior reporter." Junie glances at the TV. Another commercial. "So Amber's lukewarm on him now."

A week? That doesn't sound like it'd fit into the agenda of a rhino killer. I guess that just makes Rob a rude reporter with a large forehead and too much hair gel. Now we're down to Damon and Chef L'Oeuf for suspects.

"Amber's going back to the set tomorrow around noon," Junie says, an eye still on the TV screen. "You wanna do something together?"

"Sorry. I'm hooking up with Josh."

Click. The TV screen goes black. Junie squeals. "Cough up the details, girlfriend!"

chapter

29

I am a really excellent sleeper. I can crash anywhere. I can doze way late into the afternoon. I can usually sleep through high levels of noise.

So I'm totally shocked on Tuesday to find myself leaping out of bed at the crack of dawn. I glance at the digital alarm clock and shake my head. Nine thirty-two a.m. What is going on?

And that's when I hear it. Loud, obnoxious squawking from Grandpa at my bedroom window and loud, obnoxious squawking from Amber at my bedroom door. It's like I'm in a pet store. Where the animals are revolting.

"Shut that bird up!" Amber yells. "Shut it up!"

Squawk. Squawk. Squawk.

"Shut up!"

Of the two, Amber wins the Shriek Award.

Sighing heavily, I open the door.

All puffy-eyed, she elbows past me. "I'm gonna kill that freakin' bird. I gotta have my sleep. I'm gonna kill that bird."

Behind her, Junie stumbles into the room, hiking up her Mickey Mouse pajama bottoms.

We owl-blink at each other and yawn.

Amber beelines to the window and tugs it open.

Grandpa screeches loud and high. He flies at the screen, then lifts up backward, kicking his scrawny little feet at Amber. He's, like, totally teasing her.

With a push, she flips the screen out, shoving it down to the ground. Then she leans way out through the open space, both arms outstretched, trying to grab Grandpa. "Come here, you maniac bird. You wanna piece of me? Come and get it." All mafia-like, she's waving him in, her nail jewels glinting in the early-morning sun. "You wanna piece of me?"

Grandpa coasts in close, hovers above her just out of reach, then drops a big, fat, juicy one. Right on the top of her head.

"Ahhhhhhhhhh!" Amber's scream rattles the ceiling fan. Then she's outta the bedroom and into the shower before the ringing in my ears has stopped.

"Sherry?" Junie says, a puzzled look on her face. "Is that the same bird from the Wild Animal Park?"

"Yeah." Crossing my arms, I stick my head out the window. "Grandpa, that wasn't very mature."

167

He flaps over to a nearby bush and cackles.

A sudden breeze whips up, carrying on it the smell of coffee. The grass flattens as my mother skids in.

The corner of the screen pops into the air. "Can you help me with this?" Mom asks, all nice, obviously wanting to get along.

"Sure." I can be nice too.

Junie's as white as a ghost. Her freckles are so standing out, it looks like I could pluck them off her skin.

"My mom wants us to put the screen back in."

Like she's in a trance, Junie moves to the window.

The screen floats toward us. I grasp the sides, and Junie slots the bottom into the metal track. From the outside, Mom jiggles the top till it slides into place, and Grandpa head-nudges the screen sideways till it's gliding nice and smooth.

We're quite the little team. Although one of us looks like her 4.0 mind is being blown wide open.

"Thank you, Sherry," my mom says. "Tell Junie thank you for me."

"My mom says thanks," I say to Junie, my eyes on her every reaction. "I'm passing along the message 'cause no one can hear her but me."

Her tongue tip is poking out between her teeth, a signal that Junie is hard-core processing.

Mom says, "Grandpa wants to meet on the patio."

"Sure thing, Mom. Just let me throw on some clothes." I open my suitcase. "Junie, wanna join Grandpa, Mom and me on the patio?"

No answer.

The bedroom door creaks.

I turn around just in time to catch sight of Junie's Mickey Mouse butt leaving the room.

I get dressed, then head down the hall to the kitchen and grab a Mountain Dew Code Red from the fridge. My stomach's nervous-jumpy. I really thought I didn't care if Junie believed me or not. I mean, I'm in it for my mom. But now that there's a little sliver of a chance that Junie might join me, truly join me, in this strange adventure, I want it so bad. It's like when you get the flu and your whole body aches. I ache all over with how bad I want my best friend and me to be on the same wavelength.

I step out onto the patio.

No Junie.

"Over here, Sherry." Mom's voice comes from one of the flowered garden chairs.

Plunking my soda down on the table, I sink into the chair across from her. I pop the tab and slurp.

No Junie.

Grandpa croaks, "Get talking, girls." Or else it was, "Pet-walking squirrels." Or maybe, "Bet on mock turtles."

No Junie.

Mom clears her throat. "You know, Sherry, I probably didn't always make the best choices in life. Certainly there were times when I picked work over home. And if I could redo that last shift . . ." She draws in a ragged breath. "I would." More throat clearing. "You and your brother are the best things that ever happened to me. And this time that I'm getting with you now is really precious."

I'm all teary-eyed.

And then I feel pressure on my shoulders. A hugging kind of pressure. My mom's hugging me. And I'm feeling it.

I whisper, "I love you, Mom."

"I love you too, Sherry."

Grandpa hiccups. His eyes glisten.

"We love you too, Grandpa," I choke out.

The cushion on the chair smushes as my mother sits back down. "Have you heard from your dad? How's Sam doing?" Her voice catches on my brother's name.

"I guess Sam's driving Grandma crazy. She signed him up for some lame math camp."

"Sam and his math," Mom says, all proud.

I roll my eyes. I am not up for hearing about the extraordinary braininess of my little brother. So I launch into how we should investigate Damon when we're finished at the restaurant.

Grandpa says something long and mumbo-jumbo-ish. I don't catch a single word of it.

"I agree," Mom says.

"What?" I ask. "What's going on?"

"The timing is too tight for us all to stay together. And I, um, still need your grandfather to play navigator," Mom says. "We think you should investigate at the restaurant while we check out Damon."

No, no, no. I want a teamwork day. "You said before you'd come with me," I moan.

"It's just not working out, pumpkin," Mom says. "You can definitely handle the restaurant. The main thing is to lay low while you're there."

"I don't want to lay low all by myself."

"Chef L'Oeuf doesn't have a police record. He has absolutely no history of violence. He's got a high turnover of staff, so he's used to seeing new faces," she says. "The whole restaurant situation is completely safe."

"Even if it's completely safe, I don't want to go by myself."

"Keep your eyes and ears open. Do some snooping when the coast is clear. Is there anything indicating the type of evening planned? Like decorations? Are there any recipes for wild game? Any suspicious receipts?

"Whatever you do," Mom continues, "don't draw attention to yourself. Let's keep him in the dark about his potential-suspect status. We want the element of surprise on our side."

"I'm not sure if I'm coming through loud and clear." I turn up the whine. "I'm not going to the restaurant by myself."

"Be there at three o'clock," Mom says.

"I really, really, really don't want—"

"I'll go with you, Sherry." Junie's leaning against the patio door.

chapter 30

When the meeting's over, Junie and I raid my aunt's freezer. Over waffles and a boatload of syrup, I pretty much bring her up to speed on the mystery.

"Sherry"—she pauses—"I'm sorry about the way I've been." Her face goes splotchy. "Paranormal elements really aren't my thing, you know." Her face goes splotchier. "But I should've trusted you, and I didn't."

I stand there biting my bottom lip, twirling my hair around my finger. Like a court-jester Halloween costume, I'm two different things all at the same time. I'm relieved and resentful.

I'm relieved because Junie's my best friend, and now we can be a unit again, and she can help me solve the mystery. I'm resentful because she's been so mean.

I bite my lip some more and twirl my hair into a knot.

She lunges at me, enveloping me in a big hug.

I'm all stiff, like wood. I want to scream "I told you so!" Instead, I relax and hug her back.

"I will never, ever let you down again." Junie pinky-promises me. "Give me an assignment, something to investigate. I'll prove it to you."

"Well, my next problem is how I'm going to get to all the different places this afternoon," I say.

"Piece of cake." Junie counts off on her fingers. "Amber can drop you off at the amusement park, then go to her movie shoot, then pick you up and bring you back here in time for you to give me the scoop on Josh, and then she can drive us both to the restaurant."

Junie has seriously lost her mind if she believes Amber's gonna go for this plan. This thought must show on my face.

"Sherry, trust me. It'll work." She calls out, "Amber!"

Amber waltzes into the kitchen. She's wearing her new halter dress. "Is my breakfast ready yet, Junie?"

"Not exactly," Junie says. "Remember the time you spent the night at my house? Technically, you were grounded, but you snuck out the window at midnight to hang with Sean Franklin's older brother. The brother with the motorcycle."

Amber crosses her arms. "Kind of."

Junie reels off the driving itinerary.

Amber doesn't say a word. She stomps to the cupboard, clatters a cereal bowl onto the counter and dumps in Froot Loops and milk. Her jaw jumps up and down with each savage chew.

chapter

31

Amber barely slows down to drop me off at Belmont Park. For a girl who's überly into boys, she's not very helpful when it comes to the rest of us.

I wait a few footsteps inside the entrance gate, soaking up the atmosphere, getting my bearings. I'm taking a couple of minutes to get into the cool-date-with-cute-guy groove. Trying to ignore the basketball-sized nervousness in my stomach.

I'm very adorably dressed in my good-luck capri jeans with a wide belt, my good-luck plum-colored baby-doll top and my good-luck plum-colored flip-flops.

The perfect number of people are milling around. Enough to make it fun but not so many that there'll be long lines for the rides. Under chattering voices and screams from the roller coaster, there's a hum of nonstop carney patter. "Step right up, folks. Try your luck at Water Gun Fun, where everyone's a winner." And I'm totally loving the fried, sugary funnel-cake smell.

I catch sight of Josh by the ticket booth. He pulls a hand out of his shorts pocket to adjust his sunglasses, then sits on a low wall, legs stretched out. Maybe he's getting in the date groove too?

He glances around, sees me and waves me over.

There's a butterfly convention in my stomach.

"Hi, Sherry!" His smile's a little shaky. "It's kinda weird seeing you here."

He's right; it *is* kinda weird meeting up away from good old Saguaro Middle School. I nod, unsure of whether my voice'll come out as a squeak or not. Like the basketball's trying to bounce up into my throat.

"Ya wanna get wristbands?" Josh points to the sign.

I glance at the price. Good thing my dad gave me spending money. "Sure."

"We gotta ride the Giant Dipper. The roller coaster," he says. "It's famous from being in radio contests. Like, whoever stayed on longest won a car or a load of money."

After buying wristbands, we head straight to the roller coaster. Next thing I know, we're in a teal-colored car, clackety-clacking along faded wooden tracks. Suddenly, we shoot into darkness. With a jolt, we're wrenched back into blinding sunlight, climbing up, up, up. We teeter at the top. We plunge. I scream. Bashed around the car, my bones rattle. I grit my teeth. My head slams against the headrest. I scream again. Bruises are popping up all over my body.

We lurch to a stop. I carefully clamber out, straightening my spine, massaging my hip.

By far, that's the jerkiest, roughest, most painful roller coaster I've ever ridden. I literally hurt everywhere. To the point I need Extra Strength Tylenol.

I was thrown against Josh Morton thirteen times.

"Let's go again," I say.

After, like, three rides on the Giant Dipper, which translates into thirty-nine collisions with Josh, he says, rubbing his elbow, "Wanna try our luck at the midway games?"

"Yeah." One more ride on that roller coaster, and I'll probably have a concussion. And you know what? Chilling with Josh in San Diego isn't feeling weird anymore. It's feeling fun.

Josh's eyes light up in front of Down the Clown. Holding out some money, he says, "I'll take a bucket of balls."

The carney plunks the bucket on the counter. "Good luck."

Josh grabs a ball, squeezes it, rolls it around in the palm of his hand. He raises an arm, squints—and *wham!*

One clown head is down for the count.

Wham! Wham! Wham!

Three more clown heads bite the dust.

"Wow," I say. "You're awesome."

"Thanks." Josh lowers his arm. His blue eyes sparkle at me. "Water polo."

He raises his arm again.

More whams. More flattened clown heads. A crowd gathers behind us. "That guy hasn't missed yet." "He's incredible." "What an arm."

I turn and smile at Josh's admirers. "He plays water polo."

You know you've found an awesome guy when you're walking around Belmont Park clutching five stuffed Shamus. Other girls eye me with envy.

We pass a game called Coconut Climb. I tug on Josh's arm. "That looks interesting."

He says, "Go for it."

And I do. The carney straps me into a harness. I kick off my sandals, wipe my hands on my capris, and get a foothold at the bottom of the plastic palm-tree trunk. I scramble to the top like a mountain goat, smack the red button, then rappel down.

"Cool." Josh's eyes are all wide and impressed.

I scale the fake tree a bunch more times and win five inflatable monkeys for Josh. Climbing the pear tree in my backyard has turned me into a Coconut Climb champion.

We're such big winners, I'm surprised the park doesn't ask us to leave. In order to give other people a chance.

Somehow, amid all the Shamus and monkeys, Josh grabs my hand and pulls me over to the churro cart. We're laughing and juggling prizes and sharing a giant churro and a jumbo frozen lemonade. My hand is tingling from where it made contact with his hand.

Josh sips from the straw, then hands me the cup.

As the freezing-cold slush slides down my throat, a thought slides into my brain. Belmont Park is an important and life-altering experience. Because now I have a first-date connection with Josh Morton. And he has one with me.

I'm slurping on the lemonade, feeling it all icy on my tongue, sharing Josh's straw, thinking how it's the best, most perfect first date.

And then an unpleasant thing happens. And that unpleasant thing is named Amber.

chapter 32

It's around three o'clock, and Junie and I are at the restaurant, chilling on the sidewalk, toe-poking the rubbery tar between two squares. Behind us is an unlit On the Bay sign with wavy blue letters. We're feeling pretty confident because there's two of us.

We continue dissecting my date with Josh.

"I still can't believe Amber picked you up a whole hour early," Junie says.

"I was so bummed," I say. "I just know Josh was planning to hold my hand again." I explain in Junie terms. "Mathematically speaking, we'd been there for two hours and he held my hand once. If we'd stayed another two hours, he'd definitely have held my hand at least one more time."

"Makes sense," she says. "So, when are you getting together again?"

"He's gonna call me Thursday. Tomorrow he's gotta do family stuff with his aunt and cousins."

A guy and a girl, both tall and skinny, with long, stringy dirty-blond hair and matching Santana High School T-shirts, show up. Can you say twins? Anyway, he plunks down onto the curb, legs sticking out into the street and head bobbing to his iPod. She paces, pressing buttons on her iPod, adjusting her earbuds, checking her watch.

"*Allons-y! Allons-y!* Hurry! Hurry!" A short, paunchy man with a majorly receding hairline scuttles toward us, the tails of his white chef's coat billowing out behind him. He unlocks and whips open the front door, then waves us over with a stubby arm.

The mysterious Chef L'Oeuf has arrived.

The girl pockets her iPod and scurries to the door, while the guy folds in his legs, rubs a knee, then slowly lifts himself to a stand.

Junie and I fall into line behind him, acting all nonchalant, like one of the gang, like it's just another day at the office. Meanwhile, my stomach is tied up and scared.

As they file past the chef, he says, "*Bonjour*, Lindsey. Lindsey, get zee net for your hairs. *Bonjour*, Luke."

He stops-signs me with his hand. "I am Chef L'Oeuf. Who are yooou?" His accent's all Inspector Clouseau from *The Pink Panther*.

"Oh." And before the thought that I shouldn't give my real name is even fully formed, I pop out with, "Céline Dion."

"Céline Dion?" His eyebrows shoot up with surprise. "Like zee singer?"

"Uh, yeah. Kinda. But we're not related." I grab Junie's hand. "We're here to get credit for a career project at school. Our teacher probably called you. The Ruler? I mean, Miss Paulson? I mean, Mrs. Baldwin?" I am so thinking on my feet.

"No, no one of zeez names called me," he says. "But yooou are interested in zee food industry, Céline?"

"Sure." In the sense that I've eaten in lots of restaurants.

Grinning at me like I'm his new pet poodle, the chef pats my head and backs up so that I can squeeze past his belly. "Ah, *ma petite* Céline Dion."

Okay. I'm in.

"And yooou are who?" Chef L'Oeuf says to Junie.

She's not as quick-thinking as me. "Junie Carter. I'm doing the same career project as, uh, Céline."

We follow Luke and Lindsey across the foyer, through the dining area, to a swinging door. The whole way I can hear the chef's shoes clicking behind me, like he's some sort of cooking general.

I push through the door. We're in a long, narrow kitchen with a sharp, clean antiseptic smell. On one wall, copper-bottomed pots and utensils hang above the stoves. The opposite wall is a huge fridge with shiny stainless-steel doors. On either side of the fridge, there's a tile counter with loads of drawers under it and loads of cupboards above it.

Lindsey marches over to a drawer and yanks out a hairnet. Holding the elastic tight at her forehead, she stretches the net over the rest of her head. Then she starts poking in every single stray hair strand. This girl means serious business.

When she's satisfied with the hairnet, she zooms to another drawer and hauls out a bunch of ceramic bowls. The whole time, she's zinging little sideways glances at the chef to check if he's watching her.

Chef L'Oeuf says, "Where are zee others?"

Luke thumbs down his iPod's volume. "Surf's up, dude." He shakes his head. "Bummer for me. With a broke board."

Frowning, the chef lets loose a torrent of French vowels and consonants. I pick out "California" and "imbeciles." I'm pretty sure it's the whole work-ethic lecture. My dad can blast off a killer one in English.

Lindsey unhooks a skillet the size of the Grand Canyon and clatters it onto a stove top.

"*Avec l'amour,* Lindsey." Chef L'Oeuf tsks. "Wiz love. Zees is why you are not yet successful wiz your special dish. You must create wiz love."

She stiffens.

He turns to me and purses his lips, pushing them in and out like they're doing exercises. Then he hums some Céline Dion. Finally, he snaps his fingers. "Meringue."

Meringue? What's he talking about? My chest is tight like a Lycra T-shirt.

Eyes still on me, Chef L'Oeuf says, "Lindsey, get Céline started. I have zee good feeling about her as zee meringue sous-chef. Zee very good feeling. *Oui. Oui.*"

Yikes. One look at Lindsey, and I can see she definitely doesn't

have "zee good feeling" about me. And excuse my culinary igno-
rance, but isn't meringue a dance with a lot of hip action?

The chef considers Junie. "Zee silverware. You can polish."

Junie's face falls.

When she passes me, I whisper in her ear, "Remember, this isn't
a real job. We're here to investigate." As the meringue sous-chef,
I can afford to be generous.

"Luke." The chef head-gestures to the back door. "Let us carry
in the *mesabs*."

They leave.

"What are *mesabs*?" I ask.

Lindsey looks up from where she's hunched over a deep drawer,
hugging a huge glass bowl to her chest. "Wicker tables." Her legs
all bowed with the effort, she staggers over to me and deposits
the bowl on the counter. "There's stools to go with them too.
Covered with monkey fur."

"Yuck."

"Yuck?" Lindsey makes a face at me like I've sprouted an extra
head. "You're like my brother. You just don't get Chef L'Oeuf."
Now she's slapping down measuring cups and a grinder next to
the bowl. "Chef L'Oeuf is a brilliant artist. He's creating the most
perfect African evening ever."

My heart thumps wildly like a bunch of bongo drums. I gulp.
"And, uh, what's the main meat dish?"

Junie stops polishing mid spoon.

"Céline." Lindsey hmpfs. "Only Chef L'Oeuf has the big picture.
I just need to get my part under control."

"Which is what?" Besides being nutcase extraordinaire.

"*Injera*. It's an edible tablecloth made of a sourdough pancake bread. You tear a piece off and wrap your food in it. Like mini burritos."

"Sounds . . . interesting."

"Yeah, if I could just nail it." Lindsey's eyes well up. "It's really, really tricky. Especially because we don't have the right kind of flour in America." She blinks back tears.

That's a lot of emotion for an edible tablecloth.

"I don't want to let Chef L'Oeuf down." She sniffs. "I have to wow him so he'll sign me up as one of his specials. You know, the sous-chefs he flies in the night before."

The sous-chefs he flies in the night before? Does this secret club include rhino cooks?

"What's the deal with the meringue?" I ask. "As in, what is the stuff?"

"It's for lemon-meringue pie. The chef *must* serve it. It's in every restaurant in South Africa."

Ahhh. I get it. Meringue is that fluffy whitish-beigish junk on the top of lemon-meringue pies.

"The big problem is getting it to peak," Lindsey says.

Are we talking mountain climbing or baking?

"No one's been able to get it to stiffen properly. Chef L'Oeuf thinks we might be too close to the ocean." Lindsey crosses her arms. "But he obviously thinks you're the special meringue girl." Her eyes flash jealousy at me.

I nod big, pretending like it's majorly exciting. I'm so not the meringue girl. I'm a Fearless Rhino Warrior, here to determine if

Chef L'Oeuf plans to serve rhino meat. And then my mom, my grandpa, Junie and me will shut him down.

Junie drops a handful of forks.

"Careful. You need to polish with love," Lindsey says.

I catch Junie's eye and wink. She winks back. I'm so digging team sleuthing with her.

Lindsey jets from drawer to drawer and cupboard to cupboard, gathering items for my station. Cream of tartar. Sugar. Eggs.

"I better get to know my way around the kitchen," I say. "You don't need to keep getting my stuff out. Not with the *injera*-tablecloth thing to deal with."

Her jaw drops in surprise. She's so used to being a peon. "Works for me." She moves back to her own station and plunges her arms into a bowl of flour.

"Lindsey?" I give her a thumb's-up. "Your tablecloth'll be a hit."

With a hint of a smile on her face, she drips water into her mixture.

"Hey, Junie." With my hand, I mime talking.

She gives me the thumb's-up, grabs a bunch of silverware and her polishing rag and goes over to Lindsey. "How'd you get into cooking? Was it through your high school?"

So, where to start snooping? I walk to one end of the kitchen and start pulling out drawers. Nothing but kitchen junk. In fact, looking around, I can see there's a lot of kitchen junk in this kitchen.

I'm on my hands and knees, holding my breath against a moldy, mildewy smell, peering under the sink, when I find it. An old, battered leather briefcase with a dog-eared tag around the handle: ANDRÉ L'OEUF.

I poke my head out for a peek at Lindsey. She's kneading away, pounding the life out of a hunk of dough. In between whacks, she chats with Junie. No Chef L'Oeuf or Luke either. They're still playing moving men.

The coast is clear.

Back under the sink, I squeeze the ancient, tarnished clasp, and the briefcase accordion-opens. I start leafing through the loose papers. In the first section, there's a bunch of newspaper articles with Chef L'Oeuf's name in the headlines, and another chef's name too, Chef Poulet. Unfortunately, the articles are in French. At least, I think it's French. There's a bunch of accent marks.

I hit pay dirt with the last article which is, yay, in civilized English. I scan it.

Basically, Chef Poulet, from some place called Brussels, wants to topple Chef L'Oeuf from king of the culinary heap. Chef Poulet comes from a way-rich family and has oodles of money and says he can create theme evenings even more extravagant and exotic than Chef L'Oeuf's. And Chef Poulet is opening his own exclusive restaurant in Paris. Chef L'Oeuf says he's opening his own Parisian restaurant too. Some people in the restaurant world question where he's scoring the money. Then Chef L'Oeuf brags about how incredible this year's theme dinner will be.

By the end of the article, I'm feeling proud and sick at the same time. I'm proud because I discovered important stuff. Motive stuff. An African theme evening with rhino meat would so work for Chef L'Oeuf, who needs bags of money. I feel sick at the thought of people eating rhino meat.

I stuff the article in the briefcase and put everything back the way I found it. In the nick of time.

Charging through the swinging door, Chef L'Oeuf yells, "You are imbecile. You are surfing idiot."

Luke slouches through the door.

No *mesabs* in sight.

"Grab many of zee dish towels!" the chef shouts. "You will protect zee table corners wiz zeez."

I back out fast from under the sink, bumping my head on a pipe. "Ouch!"

The chef barks at me, "What are yooou doing?"

chapter 33

Teeth clamped together, I ignore the throbbing head pain and give my best suck-up smile. "Just familiarizing myself with the kitchen." I nod like I'm cool and in control. Meanwhile, sweat's running down my sides. "Getting in the groove so I can whip up meringue with love. And I'm feeling it. Feeling the love."

"Vraiment?" He crosses his arms over his big belly. "Really?" He stares at me, trying to decide how much of my act is for real.

I hum a little Céline, then wiggle my fingertips in the air. "I'm feeling very meringue-y."

"Vite, vite, quick, quick." He helps me to my feet. "To the counter. You must make zee meringue."

I scamper to my station.

"As for you," he says to Luke, "you are useless wiz the skinny door, knocking off a corner of a *mesab*. Now you will carry every table and every furry stool through the wide front door."

Luke groans.

"Joonie, you help him."

"Yes, sir," Junie says. If there are any additional clues to be found, she'll find them.

I can't wait to tell her about the article.

Straight-armed, Chef L'Oeuf points. "Go! Both of you!"

Luke shuffles out. Junie follows. There's a spring in her step. She's glad to be off polishing duty and on to an activity that calls for brains.

Lindsey keeps on wrestling with her dough.

I pop open the egg carton and gasp. The eggs have all turned brown.

At my side, Chef L'Oeuf says, "Beautiful, aren't zey? Zee organic eggs will form zee high, fluffy peaks."

I have truly entered a weird and wacky world. Where eggs are brown.

Next to me and practically right under a No Smoking sign, Chef L'Oeuf pulls a soft pack and a lighter from a secret pocket inside his chef's jacket, then tweezers out a cigarette with his pointy-like-candy-corn teeth. With a quick flick, he lights his cigarette.

I guess my eyes are totally bugging out, because he says, all haughty, "I am ZEE Chef L'Oeuf, *ma petite* Céline. Zee rules do not apply."

Wow. Stir that attitude in with the articles about how Friday's

189

dinner has to be over-the-top, and you have a recipe for rhino disaster.

Cigarette dangling from his lips, the chef picks up the grinder.

I cough. What a foul, disgusting odor, like burning rubber.

"*Gauloises*," he says. "I carry zee cigarettes wiz me from *la France*."

Why?

Now Chef L'Oeuf is grinding sugar into the big bowl. And the air reeks of sweetness and tobacco mixed together.

"*Le sucre,* the sugar, it must be *très, très* dissolvable," he says. This leads to a megaboring lecture about refined sugar versus castor sugar and how I have to drizzle the sugar into the egg whites while beating. And how I'm aiming for egg foam. Next he's cracking eggs on the side of the bowl and plopping the yolks into a little bowl and the whites into the big bowl while droning on about Gasparini, some pastry dude who invented meringue a million years ago. And how Marie Antoinette made hers with her own little hands.

The whole time the chef's working and talking in half French, half English, the cigarette wags between his lips. Amazingly, the ash never plops on any food.

Then, in a moment of complete silence, he holds out these archaic hand beaters to me like he's bequeathing the royal jewels. "Zee *très, très* special meringue beaters. To help you wiz your magic, Céline."

I drizzle in sugar. I beat.

He leaves the kitchen to check on Luke and Junie.

I drizzle. I beat.

He returns and checks on Lindsey.

I drizzle. I beat.

He checks on me.

Nothing peaking.

"I forget zee music." The chef pops a CD into a portable player and positions the speakers so that they're blaring drumbeats and some flutish instrument right at my bowl.

I drizzle. I beat.

My arms and wrists and hands feel like they're going to fall off and splatter right into the bowl of stubborn, flat egg whites.

I drizzle. I beat.

I am so achy that my entire upper body is going numb. Not to mention the three humongous blisters on my right foot that haven't had a chance to heal.

The chef's cell phone bursts into a Celine Dion song. Of course. *"Allô."*

"One minute," the chef says. "I need zee privacy." He goes into the broom closet.

Like that's not suspicious. I glance at Lindsey to make sure she's still communing with her dough, prop my beaters up against the side of the bowl, crank the music volume to cover up the lack of beater noise, then tiptoe to the closet.

I press my ear to the door. Ouch. Obviously they don't believe in whispering in France. I step back.

"Repeat, please," Chef L'Oeuf says in his loud, French voice. "I cannot understand your strange accent."

He's making accent comments? Now, that's just wrong.

"*Oui, oui,*" he says. "I will take both zee rhino meat and zee horn."

Ack. Eek.

"*Oui, oui,* you will receive zee bigger percentage. *Bien sûr.* Zees is a *très* good deal for zee two of us."

He's talking to the poacher.

There's a pause, and then he says, "*Oui, oui,* Thursday night is good. I need zee fresh meat for Friday."

Ack. Help. The poacher's going for it in two nights.

There's another pause. "Just don't tell them," the chef says.

Clatter. Bang. Boom. Loud, scary sounds are happening in the dining area.

The chef bursts out of the closet. "I call you back. I call you back."

His heavy footsteps thump past me. Then I hear him bang open the swinging door to the dining area. The sec the swinging door clangs shut, I unflatten myself from the wall and slowly close the closet door. A shiny object lies on the linoleum floor. The chef's cell. In his panicky hurry, he must've dropped it.

I have to grab it. But I'm frozen. Of course. I try to lift my right foot. No go. I try to lift my left foot. No go. I am so sick of this freezing problem. The phone. The phone. I have to have it. It's the key to the case. I think of cute little Ongava and the female crash and how they're counting on me. I think of my mother and how horrible it would be to lose her again and how she's counting on me.

And all those thoughts do the trick. I look around, acting all together and relaxed. Lindsey is punching her dough, really whomping it.

I dash over and snatch up the phone. While jabbing keypad buttons like I'm crazed, I dart back to my station.

What is with this phone? Where's the Calls Received screen?

The swinging door opens, and the chef strides to the counter, shouting over his shoulder, "Luke, yooou touch nothing. Yooou moron. Joonie, don't let him touch anything."

Hands on hips, he stares around the area where he accidentally dropped his phone. He blinks. He opens the closet door and looks inside. Shaking his head, he slaps his pockets. "Céline?"

Yikes. Yikes. Yikes.

He's steamrolling toward me.

I totally panic and sink the cell into my bowl. I'll never get the poacher's number off it now.

I drizzle. I beat.

"Deed you see my telephone?"

"Um, um, um."

The chef looks in my bowl. His jaw drops. *Mon Dieu!*

Mon Dieu indeed. Beautiful, tall, snow white peaks rise proud and firm. Like mini-mountains, they point to the ceiling. They stand at attention. They're perfect and gorgeous. I, Sherlock Holmes Baldwin, aka Céline Dion, have produced the meringue of all meringues.

"Lindsey!" Chef L'Oeuf calls. Then he waddles as quickly as he can to the door and shouts, "Luke! Joonie!"

Back by my side, he pats my head. "Céline, yooou are zee most talented sous-chef of meringue in the United States of America. Maybe even in *la France*."

"*Merci*," I say. "Thanks."

193

"Good job, Céline," Lindsey says.

Luke and Junie skid in.

"Way cool, dude." Luke whistles.

"Incredible," Junie says.

As we're all oohing and aahing over my meringue brilliance, the peaks start swaying and gurgling and foaming. The tallest, most amazing peak slowly sinks, toppling with a plop. The other peaks follow suit. Then, from the depths of the dancing, bubbling mixture, a song warbles up. At first, it's low and quiet, but in seconds, Céline Dion and some guy are belting out "Beauty and the Beast."

Incoming call!

chapter 34

Like we planned this morning, Mom, Grandpa and me are having an evening debriefing session on Great-aunt Margaret's porch. Junie's with us too. I'm filling them in on my restaurant fiasco and getting the lowdown on what they learned about Damon.

"Why didn't I stick the phone in my pocket?" I press my forehead onto the cool glass tabletop. "The bowl? What was I thinking? We could've had the poacher's phone number. Maybe even his name too."

"Sherry, you made a split-second decision," Mom says. "It's done. You can't beat yourself up over it."

"It could've been a restricted number," Junie says to me, "which wouldn't have given us any info."

I hadn't thought of that.

Buuurp.

Junie makes a grossed-out face.

That *was* a bijormous burp, for a small bird.

Grandpa's on the stucco wall, flapping all bizarre, with one wing fluttering forward while the other's swinging back. Very Claymation.

"You got the chef's motive. He needs money to beat out Chef Poulet," Mom says. "Thanks to you, we know Chef L'Oeuf is our man."

Yeah, thanks to me, we know Chef L'Oeuf is our man. I straighten up, moving into proud mode.

"Most police work leads to a dead end," Mom continues. "Take Grandpa and me today. We spent hours tailing Damon and then learned that legit funding came through for his movie. In fact, it was a lot of money, so he has no need to make money by killing the rhinos."

Yeah, thanks to me, we know Chef L'Oeuf is our man. I flip my hair.

Junie's watching me, all quizzical. I forget she can't hear what my mom's saying. I tell her about Damon getting a bunch of money for his movie.

"That'll make Amber happy," Junie says, "especially if it means she gets more screen time and a line."

Grandpa croaks out a bunch of gibberish and punctuates it with another scary burp.

"I'm very proud of Sherry too, Wilhelm," Mom says.

Obviously, I rock. The cell phone thing was just a small

miscalculation. I high-five Junie. I smile big across the table at Mom. Then I turn to flash an ear-to-ear grin at Grandpa.

He's asleep, his little head tucked under his little wing. He snorts out a nasally snore.

"I'm worried about your grandfather. He must be exhausted," Mom says. "Flapping from Phoenix and up to the Wild Animal Park was a long haul for him. Also, he's been flying local reconnaissance, getting to know the lay of the land."

"While he's napping, what's next for us?" I rub my shoulder. "A Jacuzzi sounds like the hot ticket after all that meringue beating." I pretzel-twist down to massage my calf. "Plus, I hiked three million miles in sandals yesterday."

Ignoring my pain, she says, "Is there any way you can spend more time at the restaurant? See if you uncover anything on the poacher's identity?"

"No!" I screech. "I deep-sixed the chef's cell in egg whites and sugar. Me and Junie hightailed it outta On the Bay so fast our heels were smoking. I'm never showing my face there again. Even if it's the last restaurant open on Earth. And I only have dirt and worms to eat and my own saliva to drink."

Junie's also looking freaked at the idea of going back to the restaurant.

"I get it, Sherry." Mom sighs. "Tell me about the phone call. All the details you can remember."

All the details? I choose a few strands of hair and start twirling. Who knew there'd be a test? "Chef L'Oeuf wants the meat and the horn. I already told you that." Twirl. Twirl. Twirl. "And he'll give the poacher more money."

"Anything else?"

I twirl a bunch more hair—like, half my head. Was there something else? Maybe. It's kinda like trying to remember a dream. "Maybe." I shake my head. "He coulda said more. But maybe not."

"If you remember something, Sherry, tell me." I bet Mom's twirling her hair too. "Did Junie hear anything?"

"No, she wasn't in the kitchen at the time." I tell Junie, "My mom's asking about the phone call."

Junie nods. "That's when I was stuck moving furniture."

Hands behind her ears, Junie's listening intently. She frowns with frustration. "I can't hear a thing."

"Sorry," I say to her. To my mom, I say, "Where do we go next?"

"When you're stuck in an investigation, always return to the scene of the crime," Mom says.

I look up at Grandpa, snoring peacefully, claws gripping a branch. "What about Grandpa?"

"He needs his sleep," Mom says. "Where's Amber? She can drive you two to the Park. I'll meet you there."

I translate for Junie, who pulls out her cell. "There's not much point in going now," she says. "Doesn't the Park close soon?"

See why she gets all As? The girl never takes a vacation from thinking.

Junie doesn't even squeeze in "Hello" before Amber's making lots of noise in her ear.

Junie says, "My bad. I didn't know you were with someone, but Sherry and I need a ride to the Wild Animal Park tomorrow."

More noise from Amber.

"I don't need to play fair. I can rat you out about Sean Franklin's bad older brother."

More noise.

"Of course I know the Golden Rule." Junie pauses. "What kind of deal?" Her voice is wary. She closes her eyes, listening. "Fine. I'll do it." She opens her eyes. "And you'll take us to the Park tomorrow morning." She disconnects.

I raise my eyebrows. "So?"

"I have to be an extra on the set tomorrow afternoon."

"What? Why?"

"Apparently, I make Amber look good."

"So, Junie," I say, "we're off detective duty till the morning." In the snap of a finger, the blisters on my feet heal and my shoulder stops throbbing. "Are you thinking what I'm thinking?"

"Shopping!" we squeal together.

chapter 35

It's Wednesday morning, and Amber is not in a good mood. Slamming my aunt's pink Mary Kay car into drive, she scowls and mutters under her breath about babysitting and her ruined life. Anyway, that's all I pick up from the backseat. Junie's in front and is probably catching more of the muttering.

I ignore the tension in the car to admire my sweet new tank top. It's turquoise + sea green and goes great with my floral skirt. If I ever score some Keflit, I will so match my aquarium. Junie discovered the tank top on a sale rack during last night's shopping spree. Fifteen percent off. Junie loves percentages. For herself, she found silk-trimmed Bermuda shorts. Very Gap. And yay for parents who are pretty generous with vacay spending money.

About halfway up the highway to the Wild Animal Park, Junie

decides to deal with Amber's bad attitude. She winks at me, then pulls a small paper bag out of her purse. "Anyone for salt-water taffy?"

Amber stops scowling. "Sure."

Junie hands her a Harry Potter candy.

Amber thinks she's such a princess that she doesn't even say thank you. She crumples the wrapper, drops it on the car floor and pops the candy into her mouth. She chews. Her face scrunches up. "Ewww. Yuck. Ewww. Yuck." She bats at her mouth. "What is it?"

"Saltwater taffy," Junie says, all innocent. "Gross-out–style." She giggles. "Barf flavor." She grabs her stomach, she's laughing so hard.

Amber pulls over to the shoulder. "Yuck. Disgusting. Repulsive." She rolls down the window and spits out the candy. "I'm doing a U-turn."

Ack. No. I can't let a cousin squabble get in the way of saving the rhinos. "You want a yummy one to get the taste out of your mouth?"

Swiping her hand across her mouth, Amber says, "I can't trust you."

"You can. I'm not the practical joker." Which is completely true. Despite her incredible braininess, it's Junie who loves a dumb practical joke.

In between laughs, Junie tosses me the bag, and I fish out a candy, which I hand to Amber. "Banana cream pie."

With the edges of her teeth, Amber mouse-nibbles the tiniest of tastes. She chews for a sec. "This is excellent." She chews for a minute. "What else do you have?"

"Caramel cheesecake, chocolate chip, tropical punch."

"I'll take them all." Amber noses back onto the road. In the right direction.

I saved the day.

Once inside the Park, Amber follows me and Junie on the path to the rhino exhibit. She says, "We're not staying long."

Hordes of visitors are tramping past us.

"Why aren't we going that way?" Amber asks.

Junie unfolds the map-and-events pamphlet. "Everyone's headed to the bird show."

As we're rounding the curve, I see a bunch of old people clumped around the fence. I recognize Bald Man, in his wheel-chair, and Tall Lavender Lady Vera towering over Arthur, owner of the beautiful, sparkling Keflit. Wow. These are serious rhino gazers. I point them out.

"I knew there wouldn't be any cute guys," Amber says. "Total waste of my morning."

"How many cute guys do you need?" I ask.

"Seriously," Junie says. "You've already got Rob and the pool-key guy here."

"Like I only want one boyfriend at a time?" Amber rolls her eyes. "You two are so middle school."

By now, we're pretty close to the old people. They nudge each other, then shuffle away from us. Must be medication time again.

"They don't act too happy to see you," Amber says.

I'm about to respond, when who do I see trotting down the path? Gary. With his perfect wavy hair and wide shoulders, he's even more adorable than I remembered.

His twinkling eyes land on Amber, Junie and me. Well, mostly on Amber. Her eyes are twinkling too, enough to start a fire. And they're definitely on him.

"Sherry, right?" Gary says, walking over.

Amber flips her hair and, with huge hip action, moves toward Gary. "I'm Amber."

Yeesh. Could she be more obvious?

"Amber, aren't you thirsty?" Junie asks. "Maybe Gary could show you where to get a drink?"

Gary has a dorky look on his face. "It is time for my break."

"Perfect." Like an octopus, Amber latches on to Gary's elbow. "Thanks for looking out for me, little cousin."

Out of the side of her mouth, Junie says to me, "It'll be easier to look around without her."

"Brilliant move, Detective Carter," I reply under my breath.

"Gary!" Bald Man shouts grumpily. "Over here. We have questions."

"I'll catch you guys later," Gary calls. Then he and Amber leave.

The old people huddle in a circle, mumbling and grumbling. They definitely need medication.

"So, we're just nosing around, looking for anything odd?" Junie asks.

"Basically," I say. "We really need my mother here."

The words are barely out of my mouth when I get a whiff of coffee.

chapter

36

"Hi, Mom," I say.

"That was close," Mom says. "I thought I wasn't going to find you. Grandpa's feeling a little under the weather, so I came out on my own."

"We better get started," I say. "Amber won't wanna be late for the movie thing this afternoon."

"Sherry, you and I'll start at opposite ends of the fence, then fan out," Mom says. "Junie can go across the path and work back toward us. Look for anything unusual, anything out of the ordinary. This is your basic needle-in-a-haystack search."

I pass the word on to Junie.

Dropping to my hands and knees, I pat the ground along the

fence. I'm slowly crawling toward the old people, pretty hidden by all the small bushes and tall grasses.

Next to me, on the other side of the fence, there's a snurgling sound and a distinct barnyard smell. Little Ongava's scrounging up a snack. He shoots me a friendly look.

A cell phone rings. Arthur picks up. After he disconnects, there's more huddling and mumbling and grumbling.

A couple of fence sections later, I say, "Mom, my knees are getting seriously dented, and I'm finding zip."

"Nothing for me yet either." Her voice fades as she drifts back toward her end of the fence.

Junie's way far from me but looks like she's searching the way she does everything else in life. With intensity.

A breeze whistles down the savanna and lifts my hair. And my skirt. I tug down on the hem. What was I thinking, wearing a skirt for detecting? And the sandals yesterday? I have got to get organized in the detective-attire department. Something practical yet chic.

The breeze whips by again, this time stronger. It carries animal and flower smells and the old people's voices.

"He wants the meat? And the horn?" Vera sounds totally pissed.

I go all rigid, like a hunting dog when he flushes a flock of birds.

"You can't trust a Frenchman." Bald Man taps the armrest of his wheelchair. "I've said it from the beginning. The entire country's dishonest."

"Mom!" I whisper-call.

"I'm phoning him." Arthur hands his cell to Vera, who pokes in numbers with her index finger. "We don't want to overreact on something this serious. Could be just a misunderstanding."

"Make it clear he's not doing that to our precious rhinos." Vera's lavender do bobs with each word.

His knuckles chalk white, Arthur presses the phone to his ear. "He's not picking up."

"Chef L'Oeuf's avoiding us," Vera says. "On purpose."

I think of the meringue bubbling and boogying. "Mom! Get over here!" I say as loud as I dare. I look around wildly. Junie's miles off.

"I vote we move to plan B." Bald Man is still tapping away. "We'll use the gun store on Coronado. Kearny's Gun Exchange. I hear they have a hefty senior-citizen discount." Bald Man slaps his armrest. "We'll take him down tomorrow."

All the old people look around at each other, nodding.

Ack. Eek. They're planning to kill the chef.

The old people trundle, hobble, roll away from the rhino exhibit.

"Mom! Where are you?" I sniff. Nothing but animals and plants and dirt. My mother has flown the coop.

I text Junie. *Get over here quick.*

"What's going on?" Junie's all breathless from running.

I tell her. All breathless from panic. "This is so bad, Junie. I can't smell my mom anywhere. The wind must've blown her away before I could tell her what I overheard—that a bunch of crazy old people are planning to murder a chef who's planning to murder a rhino for its meat and horn." I put a hand on my chest and force myself to breathe evenly.

Junie's cell rings. "What's up, Amber?" She frowns. "No, we don't want to meet you in the parking lot in one minute." She listens some more before snapping her phone shut. "Sherry, the studio called, and this afternoon's shoot starts early. I gotta go. I promised." Closing her eyes, she leans her head back. "You're right. This *is* bad."

My mind's racing. My heart's racing. My feet are racing.

I'm ditching my mother.

A detective's gotta do what a detective's gotta do.

And I know what I have to do next.

chapter 37

Amber drives to the condo like a crazed wannabe movie star. Then she dashes around her bedroom like a crazed wannabe movie star, scooping up all her new clothes and accessories.

Meanwhile, like crazed rhino protectors, me and Junie are scrambling to brew up a cup of coffee, which I plunk on the patio table with a note that says *Kearny's Gun Exchange*. Hoping against hope my mom makes it this far. Then we're madly leafing through the phone book, hunting for the address of the gun store.

"Junie, we're leaving. As in now." Amber tugs on Junie's arm.

Junie shakes loose. "It's on Third." She chews on her tongue, thinking. "That's only a couple of miles away."

"I can't walk it." I lift my foot. "Any more blisters, and I'll be on crutches. Like, till we're in high school."

"Let's go." Amber jangles the car keys in Junie's face. "We're driving so I don't sweat."

"I'm thinking bicycle." Junie bobs her head, dodging the keys, and says to me, "There's a bike-rental place at the Del."

She is seriously the smartest friend I have.

"Rent it for a couple of days," Junie says, "in case you don't get it back before closing today."

See what I mean?

Seconds later, Amber, Junie and me're out the door and piling into my aunt's car. Then, we're there, at the Del. The engine's barely off and we're racing in our separate directions. Amber and Junie to the movie set by the pool. Me to the bike-rental place, Bells and Horns.

I barrel into Bells and Horns, skidding to a stop at the counter.

There's a blond cutie-pie with a Lance Armstrong bracelet. His badge reads: ZACH, CYCLE CONSULTANT. He winks at me but doesn't get off his cell. "Break up with her, dude," he says into the phone.

I tap on the glass countertop.

Zach catches my eye and holds up a finger. "Seriously, she's way needy. Who wants a girlfriend you have to see every day?"

I hop up and down, hoping he'll get the hint and disconnect.

"Dude, she'll still cheer for you at football games. She has to. She's a cheerleader."

"Excuse me," I interrupt. "I need a bike. Desperately."

"I gotta go, man. Customer." Zach glances at me. "Yeah, I'm at work." He pushes a piece of paper and a pen across the counter. "I know. I can't believe my dad made me get a job. So lame."

Faster than a superhero, I fill out the paperwork, pay and grab a bike and helmet. As a result, I end up with a pumpkin-colored bicycle that clashes horribly with my new tank top, and a Dora the Explorer helmet that squishes my ears and earrings into my skull.

I vault onto the bike seat and zoom off.

Behind me, Zach calls, "You training for the Tour de France?"

I'd roll my eyes, but the helmet's clamped too tightly to my head.

I pedal crazy fast, swerve into the parking lot with the Kearny's Gun Exchange sign, spring off my bike and toss it near the bike rack.

I look around, then do a double take. Kearny's is so not what I was expecting. Where's the whole western theme? Like a bunch of scraggly cacti next to a faded wooden building with a post to tie up your horse to?

Instead I'm standing in front of a strip mall. Kearny's is sandwiched between Juanita's Beauty Salon and Kragen Auto. Farther along the sidewalk, there's an In-N-Out Burger and a dentist. You can, like, get your teeth cleaned and your nails filled, then grab a cheeseburger, a set of rims and a gun. One-stop shopping.

I hit the burger joint for a coffee.

In the parking lot, there's a burgundy van with a handicapped sticker on the license plate. Must be my old people.

I spy through Kearny's security screen door. A man with short hair and an eagle tattoo on his forearm is spraying Windex on a glass counter. I wait till he's out of sight before setting the coffee next to the wall. More Mom insurance.

I slowly open the door, tiptoe in, peeking carefully around for Tattoo Man. For all I know there's an age requirement for gun stores. I'm a couple of steps into the store when a buzzer goes off, screaming my arrival.

"You looking for your grandparents?" Tattoo Man jack-in-the-boxes up from behind the counter.

"Uh, sure."

With a head jerk, he indicates the rear of the store.

When I get to the back counter, I spot them: Arthur, Tall Lavender Lady Vera and Bald Man, in his wheelchair. Waiting on them is a middle-aged man with floppy Dumbo ears and greased-down hair. They're all drooling over some weapon of future chef destruction.

I crouch down behind a big cardboard display of ammunition. Small plastic bags of bullets dangle from hooks and brush against my spine. Creepy.

"Earl, why aren't you showing us something we recognize from a cop show? Like a Glock or a SIG Sauer?" Bald Man demands. "Something with oomph."

Something with oomph?

Earl rubs an ear. "A semiautomatic isn't your smartest choice. They screw up. They jam."

"Might be a complication we should avoid," Vera says.

"Hmpf." Bald Man points a crooked finger at the display. "Which one of these two-inch-barrel revolvers is the lightest?"

Earl rubs his other ear. "Ya don't want the lightest—"

"I already explained to you about our arthritis." Bald Man is pushy.

"Ya gotta squeeze off two shots. That'll stop your garden-variety intruder." Earl shrugs. "Two shots is tough with major recoil."

Arthur and Vera take small steps away from the counter, tottering toward my hiding spot. Her purple cane taps the floor.

I curl up little like a cheese puff.

They stop, and Vera, so much taller than Arthur, slouches over him so they can get their heads together. They do make a fine couple.

Arthur shoots a look at Bald Man, who's bombarding Earl with ballistics questions. "Vera, are you sure about this?"

"I'm sure we shouldn't let the chef get away with his plan." She pats some lavender hair into place.

He sighs. "Isn't there any other way?"

"By tomorrow night?" She raises a snowy eyebrow. "Arthur, sometimes you have to take risks for what you believe in, for the future. That's what we're doing. Remember Dr. Kim."

He sighs again. They totter back to the counter.

See. They do love the rhinos. They love them so much, they're willing to take risks so the rhinos can have a future. And Dr. Kim, whoever he is, feels the same way.

A creepy smile on his face, Bald Man's weighing revolvers, one in each of his wrinkly palms. "I like this baby. The .357 Smith and Wesson five-shot." He passes the firearm to Arthur.

Arthur carefully hands the gun to Vera.

She turns it over a few times, then sets it on the counter. "Passes muster with me."

"So, what's the senior-citizen discount?" Bald Man asks.

Earl says, "We can do five percent."

"Five percent?" Bald Man shouts. "What if I were military? What if I hadn't been rejected for flat feet? What would the discount be then?"

Vera squeezes Bald Man's shoulder to calm him down. "We'll take it." She smiles at Earl. "Credit card okay?"

"Ya gotta take the written test first. Then there's a ten-day wait."

"Ten days?" Bald Man pounds the counter. "We can't wait ten days."

"Sorry, but that's the law." Earl doesn't look sorry at all. He locks everything up and heads to the front of the store.

"I got an idea." Bald Man's eyes are flashing, all bloodshot and psychotic. "We'll go into gang territory." He hits the counter again. "Buy a piece on the street."

Vera's lavender head is bobbing up and down in a yes, and she clomps her cane a couple of times. She's caught up in the maniac moment.

Even Arthur isn't telling them it's too dangerous.

I've always known grown-ups lose it in old age. I mean, look at Grandma Baldwin with her birds and her crystals. But these old people are *mucho* nuttier than any I've ever met. No way can I let them, these fellow Fearless Rhino Warriors, venture into gang country. They'd never hobble out alive. It's up to me to save them from their wacky selves.

I bounce up, knocking a few packages of bullets down from the rack, and dust myself off. Then, a friendly hand raised in greeting, I step out from behind the display. "Hi. I'm Sherry Baldwin.

213

I just want to let you know you can chill and stop stressing over the rhinos. You guys don't need a gun. You don't need to kill the chef. My mom, grandfather and me are totally on top of the situation. We'll keep our precious rhinos safe."

The three of them stop dead in their tracks.

I can tell by their glassy stares and dropped jaws that they don't know whether to believe me or not. Which makes sense. I mean, I'm only a teen who popped up unexpectedly from behind an ammunition display. "Really. We can handle it. We've been investigating, and we've got it all figured out."

Still no response from the old people. They're like statues.

"Like, for example, we know the poacher will strike tomorrow night, Thursday, because the chef's special dinner is Friday, and he wants everything, uh, fresh."

I dig in my mini-backpack and pull out a used Wild Animal Park ticket and a pen. After jotting down my cell number, I hand the ticket to Arthur. "Feel free to check in on our progress. I'm happy to keep you up-to-date."

He slowly stretches out an arm to take the number.

I beam a cupidy matchmaker's grin at him and Vera. "I happened to overhear you two planning a country-western dancing date to practice your two-step. Go for it. Have fun. No more rhino worries." I look at Bald Man. "You too. Go enjoy yourself with a normal retired-person activity, like watching bowling on TV."

Vera clutches Arthur's arm, and they navigate a huge path around me. At breakneck speed, Bald Man whips to the front door in his wheelchair.

I hear Vera say, "Who is she and where did she come from?"

Her tone of voice says, *What lunatic institution did that incredibly deranged, demented psychopath escape from?*

No, no, no. We're on the same side. I'm sane and trustworthy and likable.

I shove my pen in my backpack and zip it shut, trying to get myself together quickly to catch the old people in the parking lot.

There's a tap on my shoulder.

chapter 38

I jump about a million miles into the air.

It's Tattoo Man, and he's standing a little too close. "Yer gonna pick up the ammo you knocked off the display, right?"

"Uh, right."

I hang up all the packets of bullets and straighten them, then exit Kearny's Gun Exchange in time to see the burgundy van careening out of the parking lot and onto the street.

"Sherry!"

I jump another million miles. "Mom! You gotta quit freaking me out like that."

"Sorry, pumpkin."

I sink down onto the curb. "So, you made it from the Park to the condo and then from the condo to here?"

"Impressive, isn't it?" A few leaves are gusted away as Mom settles next to me.

"Very. Where's Grandpa?"

"Resting up for tomorrow when we catch the poacher. We'll go over those plans in a moment. But first, bring me up to speed on what happened today at the Park and where the gun store fits into everything."

So I tell her.

There's a long pause. Too long. Finally, my mom says, "Murder? You really think the old people were planning to murder the chef?"

"Absolutely. I heard them."

"Sherry, they're pretty frail. I don't see them as a physical threat to anyone. However, I'm wondering if they're connected to the case in a different way."

I cross my arms. "I heard them."

"Just listen for a second. Perhaps the old people want rhino horns for themselves. They met on an arthritis Web site. They're in a lot of pain. Rhino horns are used in a variety of quack medicines."

"No way." I stamp my foot. I hate it when my mom blows me off. "Like I already said, I heard them. They're Fearless Rhino Warriors."

"Good police work involves keeping an open mind." Mom clears her throat. "Let's talk about your role in stopping the poacher tomorrow at the Park. Your grandfather and I feel strongly that we can prevent the crime and handle any actual conflict. Our paranormal powers give us a definite edge. We'll need you to dial nine-one-one when the situation's under control. That's all, though. I'm assuming Junie will be with you?"

"She will."

217

"Good. That makes it safer. Basically, we want you and Junie hidden and out of danger."

We figure out tomorrow's meet time, then Mom leaves to go conspire with Grandpa.

All in all, I'm feeling superb. I've turned out to be a skilled detective. I rescued the old people's butts from muggings on gang turf. I discovered they were Fearless Rhino Warriors. My mom's afterlife will be saved. The rhinos will be safe. I'm totally on track with Junie. And sweet romance is percolating between me and Josh. Major sigh.

Biking back to the condo, I yawn. At my aunt's, I'll sack out and sleep uninterrupted until tomorrow morning. At which time I'll take a long, hot shower and eat a bunch of junk food for breakfast.

Then I'm going on a secret personal errand.

chapter 39

Junie and Amber had already left when I finally rolled out of bed on Thursday. Junie's note said they had to reshoot some of yesterday's scene but that she and Amber would definitely be back in time for the Wild Animal Park jaunt later this afternoon.

I park the bike and hustle into Home Depot, filled with joy and hope. Thoughts of my darling fishies fill me with warmth. I'm here for some serious aquarium shopping.

I follow the signs hanging from the ceiling until I get to the garden center, and start poking around in the fertilizer shelves. I'm humming a happy song and feeling good.

"Can I help you?"

I look up to see an older woman, rake thin, with hair the color of yellow daisies. She's tying a bow at the back of her orange Home Depot apron.

"Hi," I say with a bright smile. "I'm looking for Keflit."

She crosses her arms over her narrow chest. "What are you planning to do with Keflit?"

I launch into the story of my turquoise + sea green bedroom walls and how I invented the paint color at Home Depot, but at a Home Depot in Phoenix—why did I pick such a tough color to match?—and how I'm trying to coordinate my aquarium decor with my walls. Okay, I know I'm rambling, but it's a pretty interesting ramble.

Arms crossed even tighter, she interrupts me with, "Do you know what Keflit is really for?"

"Planting," I say. That's one good thing about all this detective work. I've gotten really talented at remembering details. And I can totally hear Arthur saying Keflit was for planting, not aquariums.

"It used to be sold for killing weeds. Problem was, it killed a lot of other things too. And that's what it would do to your fish. Kill them."

I slap my forehead. "Kill my fish?" I absolutely do not want my precious fish floating belly-up in a delightfully decorated aquarium. I guess it's back to trying to match beads at the Hobby Shop.

"Keflit's been illegal in this country for several years now. I'm surprised you even know the name."

"Illegal?" A little ice cube of cold lodges at the base of my spine. "Why?"

"Because of how lethal it is. Even a very small amount of Keflit can kill a large animal."

"Kill a large animal?" I repeat.

She nods. "About a decade ago, they lost a couple of elephants at the Toronto Zoo because a gardener used Keflit too close to the exhibit."

"Oh no." Elephants are big. Rhinos are big. The chill creeps up my spine.

She continues, "And it works quickly. Keflit's nickname was 'two-step,' because that's how many steps an animal took before keeling over."

"Two-step?" I break out in goose bumps all over.

The pager clipped to her apron crackles. She looks at it. "Repaint your bedroom walls," she advises. "Something neutral." She leaves.

I sit down on a wooden slat, next to a tall ceramic planter. I'm freezing cold, even though it's warm out and Home Depot isn't even air conditioned but only cooled with giant, noisy ceiling fans.

I close my eyes. Around me, the smells of flowers and plants and potting soil and fertilizer all meld together and transport me to the Wild Animal Park. I'm by the fence at the rhino enclosure and I can see Arthur with the Ziploc bag of shimmering, sparkling, killing Keflit. And in my mind, as the Keflit crystals dance and glitter, pieces of the mystery puzzle slam into place. Strange snippets of phone conversations suddenly make perfect sense. I flash on sentences I interpreted as innocent when they were really sinister and murderous.

Dizzy, I grab the lip of the planter to keep from pitching into the aisle. The old people are not Fearless Rhino Warriors. Not even close. They want the rhino horn. For a funky, fringy arthritis cure.

221

Which must be where Dr. Kim comes in. My mother was right. And the old people are furious, killing furious, with the chef who went all greedy and wants the meat *and* the horn. When I was eaves-dropping at the restaurant, that's what he was talking about to the poacher. Then the weird thing he said, the thing I couldn't re-member, crashes into my consciousness. The chef said, "Just don't tell them." Meaning, don't tell the old people they're out of the rhino deal.

Shivering, I lean against the planter. I told the old people my name. I gave them my cell number. I told them Mom and Grandpa and me were protecting the rhinos. I even told them we'd be at the Park tonight. Major, major tragedy.

I'm sitting there all hunched over and hugging the planter for support. Suddenly, it's like my brain morphs into a pinball ma-chine and the poacher's name is zinging and pinging around in there. All lit up and with bells ringing. I know exactly who he is. Without a shadow of a doubt.

At Indy 500 speed, I'm out of Home Depot and on the orange rocket back to the condo. I have a huge pot of coffee to brew.

chapter

40

Just as I'm turning the key in the lock, the front door swings open.

Amber runs straight into me. She squeals.

Her clothes are so tight I'm amazed she can breathe, let alone squeal. She must have spent hours gluing them on. Her skintight gold tank top matches the polish on her toenails and fingernails, which matches her eyes. Her black jeans are molded to her. She looks awesome.

"I have a date," she says. "He's twenty-one." She rounds her index finger and thumb into an O. "And very good-looking."

Ack. Eek. "No, no, no." I'm flapping my hands in panic. "You're driving me and Junie to the Wild Animal Park."

"Nuh-uh. Junie said you guys didn't need me anymore."

Say what?

"Amber," Junie calls from inside the condo, "are you leaving?"

"I'm gonna wait at the curb!" Amber yells, heading out. "Sherry's here!"

I jet into the condo.

Galloping to the kitchen, I shout, "Why don't we need Amber? We gotta make coffee. I figured out a bunch of stuff about the mystery today. We gotta get hold of my mom and grandpa ASAP." My hands flapping even faster, I'm so nervous and scared and freaked that I can't stand still.

"Your grandfather's sick. They came by here earlier to tell you." Junie grabs a bag of Doritos. "He started feeling really crummy this morning. Your mom took him to a ghost avian specialist who gave him some medicine." She opens the bag. "But he was feeling even worse by lunchtime, so your mom's taking him back to the specialist." She pulls out a handful of chips.

"You got all that from my grandfather?" I'm impressed with Junie and worried about my grandfather all at the same time.

"I'm not saying it was easy, but you know how I've always been good with foreign languages." Junie munches on a chip. "Anyway, I'm supposed to tell you that tonight's mission is off. Your mother's exact words, according to your grandfather, were 'Sherry, tonight's mission is aborted.' He made me repeat it five times. Then he passed out."

"He passed out?"

"At least, I think that's what happened. He was standing on the patio table. Then he kind of flopped over onto his back, his feet sticking straight up in the air."

"What?"

"Then he was whooshed through the air. Over the stucco wall. And, poof—gone. I guess your mom scooped him up and rushed him to the specialist."

I slide onto a bar stool. Elbows on the counter, I hold my head up with my hands. I can't believe it. I just can't believe it. What started off as a perfect day has gone completely haywire. I close my eyes. Even though I don't know what happens to a really sick ghost bird, it can't be good. At least one rhino will die tonight. And I'll lose my mom forever. I take a deep, shuddery breath.

I freeze in that sad position for what feels like hours but is probably only seconds. During this traumatic time, I make a decision. A really tough, scary decision.

When I open my eyes, I see Junie set a Mountain Dew Code Red in front of me.

"What's your plan?" she asks. "I can tell you've got one."

Junie my best friend is so back. "The mission is not aborted. It can't be. Or I'll lose my mom forever. And rhinos will die. I'm going to the Wild Animal Park. I'm not exactly sure how, but I'm gonna stop the poacher."

"You know I'll help you."

"Junie, you're the best."

While we're loading up a big backpack, we go over our plan.

"He'll be so blown away when he sees us actually in the rhino enclosure," I say, "that he'll sorta freeze up."

"That's when you zap him in the eyes with hair spray," Junie says. "And I'll conk him on the head with the frying pan." She drops the heavy pan into the pack.

I pat my pocket with my cell. "Then I'll call the cops to come pick up a knocked-out criminal."

She pushes rope from my great-aunt's garage into the backpack, then pokes a few flashlights into a side compartment.

"I hope we can pull this off." I shake the can of Sassy Girl hair spray. Totally full. I set it in on top of the rope.

Junie zips the whole thing up.

"We gotta give it our best shot. We can't let him Keflit a rhino." I swing on my mini-backpack.

She hauls the Yellow Pages down off the bookshelf to find a taxi company.

My cell rings. It's Josh. Woohoo. The screen says Analog Roam. I'm not supposed to answer those calls. Too expensive, in The Ruler's opinion. But it's Josh. But it's analog roam. But it's—

"Hey, Josh," I say into the phone.

"Hey, Sherry, I'm free tonight. Wanna do something?"

I pause. Josh, my knight in shining armor, is available. Right when I need him most. We are so connected. We are so meant to be.

"How does a trip to the Wild Animal Park sound?" I say.

chapter 41

It's way late in the afternoon when Josh's older cousin Derek pulls into the condo parking lot. He was forced to drive us and totally glares at Junie and me as we climb into the back of his Honda. "I'm only dropping you off. Call my mom to pick you up." Derek inserts his earbuds.

"Hey, isn't that illegal?" I say loudly.

"Do you want a ride or not?" Without waiting for an answer, Derek turns on his MP3 player.

Josh shrugs, then switches from the passenger seat to the back.

Which means I'm whizzing up the highway sandwiched between Josh and Junie in a compact car. Which means my thigh is touching Josh's. At least, I think it is. Being this close to him has blown out a bunch of nerve endings, numbing my left leg.

Jostling my leg to get the feeling back, I start filling Josh in on the mystery. I'm leaving out the supernatural details. I have to. I mean, what's an acceptable amount of weirdness at the beginning of a relationship? Zero. Or less. So ixnay on the ghost stuff.

Josh says, "How'd you get involved in all this?"

" 'Cause of some people in Sherry's family." Junie's such a quick thinker now.

We're all speaking in hushed tones, although I doubt Derek can hear us over his music.

"And why aren't you going to the police?" Josh lifts a bottle of Gatorade from the cup holder and tips it back.

"We will, depending on what happens tonight."

"And what do you think'll happen?" he asks, slotting the bottle back in the holder.

"I think the poacher's gonna strike," I say. "With poison."

"And our plan is to take the last monorail ride of the day, jump down to the savanna when no one's looking, hide in the rhino enclosure and stop him?" Josh asks.

Put like that, it does sound whacked. But it is our plan, so I answer, "Well, yeah."

"And you'll recognize him?" he asks.

"Definitely."

From a case on the car floor, Josh pulls out a CD. He leans over the front seat and slides it into the player.

Derek frowns but doesn't say anything.

"You into ska?" Josh asks.

"Absolutely," Junie says.

"Ska?" I say.

Josh glances at me and grins. "Tell me what you think of this."

Punkish reggae music bounces round the car. Totally awesome, with a drumbeat that makes you want to order your almost boyfriend to pull over and show you what he knows about kissing. That is, if the driver wasn't scary-grumpy and your best friend wasn't squished up next to you.

I stretch out my neck, lean my head back and close my eyes. I block out my fears about Grandpa being super sick. I block out my fears that Josh, Junie and me are in over our heads. I block out my fears that we won't save the rhinos and my mom's afterlife. I'm grooving to the music, to sitting next to Josh, to having friends helping me.

Josh turns down the volume.

I open my eyes.

"Sneaking into the rhino enclosure and staying in the Park after closing," he says, "—how illegal is all that?"

"We're minors," Junie says. "Seems like they'd just kick us out."

Josh looks at me.

"I don't know." I'm sure he's thinking of when he hung with bad kids in San Diego and how he's being careful now. "No problem if you don't want to do it. Seriously."

"But you'll go anyway, right?" he asks.

"I have to."

"Count me in, then." He squeezes my shoulder, then cranks the volume back up.

My heart does a double twist with a somersault thingie, like one of those gymnasts at the Olympics. Josh is so there for me.

At the Wild Animal Park's main gate, I unzip the cute little outside pocket of my mini-backpack. My hand closes briefly around the crystal my grandmother gave me. I drop it back in and pull out the freebie Park tickets.

"You kids realize we close in an hour?" The employee fiddles with the latch on the booth's window and scowls. "I shouldn't even let you in."

"Please, sir." Junie smiles. "We're from out of town and might not get a chance to visit here again."

We zip through the turnstile and run to the monorail. Josh swings the big backpack with our supplies over his shoulder as he runs.

"Three more customers," he yells out to the driver-guide, who's closing all the train doors.

In true déjà vu style, the last car is empty, and we slip into it. I even look around to see if Thomas is a few rows in front, like before. Negative. The train's way less full than last time. It's dark and kinda chilly. Junie's sitting across from me. And Josh is right next to me. Our hips and thighs are touching. Yowser.

A low-hanging, round gobstopper of a moon shines weakly. Cute twinkling Christmas lights weave around the roof of the train, while glaring floodlights attached to the sides light up the landscape. I stare out over the savanna, all eerie with shadows of animals and bushes and trees. I can smell an herbally plant that must be blossoming somewhere down there.

The microphone crackles on.

I jump.

"As Alfred Hitchcock would say, good evening," our tour guide says in a deep, spooky voice. "Welcome to today's last ride. I'm Stephen, and I'll be leading you on this nocturnal adventure."

The train lurches away from the station.

Josh slides closer to me.

Is he going to hold my hand again? I wipe my palm on my jeans.

Stephen dives into an animal-facts spiel.

I tune out and force myself to think. About how I better totally get it together. My mom and the rhinos are counting on me. I can't let myself turn mushy-brained because of Josh. I have to focus, focus, focus.

The train crawls around a curve, and the floodlights beam on Ongava, standing by a palm tree. He looks up and smiles at me. He does. I swear.

I sniff. No Mom. I peer around. No Grandpa. Back at the condo, I left a full pot of coffee on the porch table. Under the carafe, there's a note saying where we are. All in the crazy hope Grandpa makes a speedy recovery and he and my mom come looking for me. I cross my fingers. I so need them to show.

The savanna is still and quiet. Even Junie's keeping her mouth shut. And I'm sure it's killing her not to add on to Stephen's animal facts. It's like we're in our own little, peaceful world up high on the tracks.

Suddenly all the lights blink out.

Someone screams. Junie. That girl is not cool.

"No need for alarm," the guide says. "I always turn off the big lights near the highway so I don't blind the drivers."

In the almost dark, the train inches forward until we're right by the rhino enclosure. I take a deep breath and whisper to Josh and Junie, "Jump. Now."

"See you down there." Josh hoists a gorgeous leg up and over the side of the train, then quickly disappears from view.

Junie crouches on the seat, then jerks a leg over the edge. For a second, it's like she's a panicky insect fighting a spiderweb, arms flailing, a leg dangling on either side. She tips over. *Thud.* Junie has landed.

Sniff. Still no sign of my mother. I squint. Still no sign of my grandfather. It's looking more and more like Grandpa's really sick and they're not gonna make it. Will he be okay? Can Josh, Junie and me truly handle tonight?

"Hang in there for a few more seconds, folks," Stephen announces, "and I'll turn the lights back on."

I'm up out of my seat and over like when the last bell rings at school the Friday before summer vacation.

Splat.

My face hits the hard dirt. The monorail lights switch on and the train whirs away. I watch the twinkling Christmas lights shrink in the distance. Civilization's driving off and leaving us in the dust.

Josh pulls me to my feet. "You okay?"

I rub my chin, hoping he didn't witness my dorky full-face landing. "I'm cool."

"What's next, Sherry?" Josh asks.

I cup my ear but don't hear any buffalo snorts. Major phew. The monster Cape buffalo must be locked up in solitary confinement, like the afternoon monorail guide promised. I look around. Above the door to the rhino hut, there's a light. And the moon's shining a little brighter. "Let's get out the flashlights."

Josh shrugs off the backpack and drops it on the ground. "They in here?"

"Zippered pocket on the right side," I say.

Junie says, "Let's separate and hide so we can watch the widest area possible. Once we locate him, we'll take him down."

"How, exactly?" Josh asks.

My insides go all jiggly and butterflyish. This is the dangerous part of our plan. "I'll call his name, and in the split second when he's super-surprised to see me, I'll squirt hair spray in his eyes, then—"

Swinging her arms over her head, Junie interrupts, "I'll knock him out with the frying pan."

"Sounds kinda dicey." Josh blows out a breath and looks at me. "Don't call his name till I'm right by you."

"Okay." I'm feeling a little less jiggly. Because I have Josh.

"Anything goes wrong, anything looks weird," he says, "we call nine-one-one right away. Okay?"

Junie and I nod.

"I wanna check out the bush at the top of the hill." Josh points. "I think it'll give me a good overview of the savanna." He pulls out the flashlights and hands one to me and one to Junie. After clicking on his light, he jogs off.

A startled antelope springs out of the way.

"Why don't you take the tree wrapped in wire?" I say to Junie, indicating a tree not too far from Josh's bush. "I'll take the feeder close to the hut, the one that looks like a giant termite cone."

Close to the hut. Close to where the banana treats were left. That's probably where the action'll take place. Yikes. But it's my mystery, my mother, my responsibility.

"Be careful, Sherry," she says, rubbing my shoulder.

Josh returns. "That's a great lookout position up there."

"How will you let us know if you see something?" Junie asks.

"I do a pretty good owl hoot," Josh says.

Wow. There's no end to this guy's talents.

We take off to our various hiding places. I flatten myself against the side of the concrete feeder. Staring into the darkness, I can make out the outline of Junie's shoulder and the top of Josh's absolutely adorable head. They seem so far off in the distance. I shiver and rub my arms.

"Mom," I whisper-call. "Grandpa."

No answer. No coffee smell. No flapping wings.

A few white goats skitter on the knoll behind Junie. They look like ghosts out on a nighttime frolic. Somewhere above me, a bird lets out a creepy call. The whole scene is überspooky.

"Hoot."

"Hoot"? I smile. Cute voice, but a really poor owl imitation.

"Hoot."

Okay, Josh, I got it. That's you being an owl.

"Hoot. Hoot. Hoot."

Oh. Oh. Oh. He sees something. He's warning me. I go nervous-twitchy all over. I look around.

"Hoot. Hoot. Hoot."

I squint. I see the fronds of a tall palm pointing like giant fingers toward the black sky. Way far off, I make out a zebra's silhouette. But nothing else.

My cell rings—more like screams—in the quiet night.

Panicked, I fumble in my pocket. I slap it off.

Footsteps.

My pulse is pounding like crazy. I drop to the ground and listen.

There's a loud click.

Ouch!

The world goes black.

chapter 42

All groggy and woozy, I slowly blink open my eyes. It's like there's a fog machine in my head, clouding everything up.

Where am I?

A skinny stream of moonlight filters through a small, dirty window. I can make out a table with several bottles of Sassy Girl shampoo. The air stinks of old food and animals.

I'm in the rhino-keeper's hut.

Through my head fog, I remember hiding by the cone-shaped feeder, Josh's pitiful hooting, my phone ringing, footsteps, a noisy click and a jab to my leg. But then what happened?

My thigh aches. I go to rub it.

Ack. I can't move my arms. I can't move my feet. I'm duct taped to a chair with my hands behind my back.

My mouth dries up like I hiked the Sonoran Desert, at noon, in the summer, without any water.

I pull against the tape. It's so tight, it squeezes me like a way-too-small Halloween mummy costume. The more I struggle, the more the tape stretches my skin and yanks on my arm hairs. And my mini-backpack is digging into my shoulder blades. My pulse speeds up. Sweat dots my forehead. Which I can't wipe off.

A major lump plugs up my throat. I swallow hard.

Peering around the hut, I see it's still a disaster area. A disaster area that's a stockpile of bad-guy supplies. There's gotta be enough duct tape to restrain Saguaro Middle School's entire student body.

I keep looking. No one except me. Are Josh and Junie out on the savanna, plotting my rescue? Through my thick head haze, I think two clear little yays.

The door squeaks open. Dressed all in black, a guy enters. Moonlight flows on and around him, lighting him up like he's a rock star on stage. But instead of a microphone, he's carrying a rifle.

Help. I'm going to die a lonely, smelly Wild Animal Park death. Josh and Junie, make the scene. Now. Pleeease.

Possumlike, I close my eyes. Surely he won't shoot me if I'm still unconscious.

In his hugely gross, creepy accent, Gary says, "Sherry, I know you're awake."

I open my eyes.

He sets the rifle on the table. "I only put a light dose of tranquilizer on the dart."

"You shot me with a dart gun?"

"Yeah." He inclines his ugly head toward the gun. "And you weren't at all difficult to track." He smirks. "You need to utilize the vibrate function on your cell phone. Or be more discerning when giving out your number."

My jaw drops. "You're the one who phoned me on the savanna?"

He nods.

Those double-crossing old people. They gave Gary my cell number.

"I knew you were out there somewhere," Gary says, "and that seemed the quickest way to pinpoint your location."

He knew I was out there? Those double-crossing blabber-mouthy old people. They told him the plans.

"Where are your mother and grandfather hiding?"

I don't answer.

"Fine. Don't talk." He shrugs. "I'll find them."

Ha. Good luck.

Gary drags a sports bag from the corner. Then he's on his haunches, shoving stuff around in the bag.

I sit perfectly still, thinking. My head's less hazy now. Whatever he shot me with is wearing off. I realize that once he starts hunting for my mom and grandpa, he'll stumble across Josh and Junie. I have to buy time for them, my two aces out on the savanna, who are waiting for the perfect moment to bust in and save me. Hopefully in time to save the rhinos too. And my mom's afterlife.

I've always been a gifted talker. I'll stall him with questions. Plus, I want the answers. "How'd you hook up with everybody?"

Gary digs some more in the bag. He hauls out some weird goggle things, which he slips around his neck. "I've done work for Dr. Kim before. The arthritics contacted him about concocting a Chinese remedy for their arthritis. A bogus remedy, I'm sure."

He zips the bag, stands and tosses it back in the corner.

Ack. Speed it up, Josh and Junie. I quickly fire out another question. "What about the chef?"

At the table, he slides a red dart from the case, then dips the pointy end of it in a small cup of liquid next to the shampoo bottles. "He knows someone in the online arthritic group. They were having trouble coming up with the horn money, so—" Gary stops talking to concentrate on slotting the dart into the back of the gun.

Ack. He's getting ready to go people hunting. "About the chef?" I ask.

He lays the gun down again, then pulls the goggles over his face.

Very Star Wars. Very night vision. Very scary.

"The chef offered to pay half if he could have the meat," Gary says.

"Why'd you leave bananas out for the rhinos?"

"To get them in the habit of checking that area. It's a good place to make the kill." He walks to the door.

I fill completely with panic. Completely. Like I'm a can of soda all shook up. "Are those night-vision goggles? I think I saw them on *CSI*." My voice shakes.

"Shut up, Sherry." He exits.

I breathe in little shallow gasps like a stupid fish who jumped

239

out of the water and is flopping around, dying on land. By now Josh and Junie must've dialed nine-one-one. Right? They must've. Which means help'll be here any minute. Help, like the whole San Diego PD. Right?

A noise outside! Yay. It's Josh, my wonderful, gorgeous knight in shining armor. Or Junie, my wonderful, full-of-great-ideas best friend. Or a bunch of cops. I'm not picky.

The door opens. Gary enters, hauling Junie over his shoulder.

It feels as though a twenty-pound block of ice is sitting on my heart, crushing it. Josh, please come through for us, and soon.

Without a word, Gary dumps Junie next to me. Her glasses bounce off. He returns to the table and dips another dart. After reloading the gun, he takes off again, leaving the door open.

Oh no. At the top of my lungs, I scream over and over, "Watch out, Josh! He's coming, Josh!"

Junie's chest rises and falls. She lies there, eyes shut. She's so out of it even my yelling doesn't wake her up.

Gary backs in, dragging Josh by the feet. Josh's head bumps along the uneven floor, his gorgeous hair swishing in the dirt. He moans.

Make that a fifty-pound block of ice. My heart is now flattened.

Gary yanks off his goggles and tosses them on the table. He unzips Junie's purse and pulls out her cell. Staring at the screen, he punches buttons, then drops the phone on the floor. He pats Josh's pockets till he finds the phone, and goes through the same routine. From the small smile on Gary's face, I can tell Josh and Junie didn't get a chance to dial nine-one-one.

It's over. Really over. Really and truly over.

Gary binds Josh's and Junie's feet and wrists. He works quickly and quietly. Turning to me, he says, "You brought these two instead of your mother and grandfather?"

My chin on my chest, I don't even bother to answer.

When he's done, he grabs the sports bag and moves to the table, shaking his head and muttering, "This should've been a relatively simple job. But dealing with those arthritics and that chef. And now these kids . . ."

His movements all jerky and angry, he unzips the bag and pulls out the Ziploc bag of Keflit. Even in the dim light, it sparkles and shimmers, beautiful and deadly at the same time.

"What's going to happen to us?" I ask, my voice thin and reedy.

"It's out of my hands."

"What does that mean?" My pitch hits girlie-girl notes. As in way high. As in way scared.

He throws me a look like I'm an annoying mosquito buzzing around his royal head. "I don't deal with complications like you guys. I'm a professional. I do my job. I get paid. I leave." From a little sink on the far wall, Gary adds water to the Keflit and squishes the mixture all around in the bag. "The guy who picks up the product is the problem solver."

"What do you mean? What's a problem solver?" I'm hysterical now.

Gary slides on disposable gloves and chooses a peeled banana. "Sherry, you've seen me. You know who I am. You've obviously confided in your friends. You do the math." He dips the end of the banana in the mixture, making sure it's coated in shimmery, glittery, turquoise + sea-green Keflit. Then, carrying a bunch of bananas, including the two-step death weapon, he exits.

I slump. Totally and completely frozen. We're doomed. The rhinos are doomed. My mother is doomed.

Right from the start, I knew I couldn't do this. I knew I was in miles over my head.

Look at me. I'm tied to a chair in a nasty old hut with a taped-up new boyfriend and a taped-up best friend. I sob big, hot, salty tears. Then my nose starts running, and I can't even lift a hand to wipe it.

I sit there, not that I can move, anyway, my eyes squeezed shut and my head hanging. This is the biggest failure of my entire life.

chapter

43

Tap. Tap. Tap.

Oh great. Now I'm getting a noisy headache from the solution El Creepo Gary dipped the darts in. I open my eyes and lift my head. It's still dark. Yellow moonlight sneaks in through the cracked door. I guess I only zoned out for a few minutes.

Tap. Tap. Tap.

My poor pounding head.

Next to me, Josh and Junie lie unconscious on the ground. Josh moans low and cute. Junie moans nasally and nerdy. If only I hadn't dragged them into the mystery.

Tap. Tap. Tap.

It sounds like tapping on glass. What kind of headache sounds like that? What kind of weirdness did Gary dart me with? Wait a sec. This is not happening inside my head. I look up. A big-bellied wren is pecking at the window.

Grandpa! He's here. He's healthy. He's my hero. I'd jump up and down with joy if I could.

"Grandpa, where's Mom?"

He stops pecking, then raises his head and stares at me. His little yellow beak opens and closes, opens and closes. He's saying . . . something.

I don't have a clue what, because I can't hear through the glass. And then there's my on-again-off-again prob with his bird talk.

"Grandpa, I can't hear you. Fly through the door. And speak slooowly."

He's back to the tap-tap-tapping thing. He stops. He raises his head. He stares. He yaks. Then he goes back to tapping again.

I sniff. I shriek, "Mom! Mom! Mom!" I sniff again. Nothing.

I turn my eyes back to Grandpa, his tiny head bobbing back and forth, his beak stabbing at the window, then opening and closing to squawk out something.

Tap. Tap. Tap.

I so don't want to die now.

Tap. Tap. Tap.

Junie and me have totally patched up our friendship.

Tap. Tap. Tap.

And then there's sweet, adorable, gorgeous Josh. We haven't even hugged yet. Or kissed.

Suddenly a coffee smell floods the hut. And a humongous feeling of relief floods me.

"Mom?" Her name catches in my throat.

"Sherry!" Her voice comes from the other side of the threshold. "I'm here, pumpkin, I'm here."

"Mom, you gotta do something!"

"Sherry, I can't get in the hut," she says, all fake calm. "You have to get yourself free."

"I've tried everything!" I cry, all freaked-out. "I'm totally taped up."

"Have you tried twisting and turning your wrist?" Still fake calm.

"I've tried everything." Still freaked-out.

Tap. Tap. Tap.

"Can you reach your ankles?" Less fake calm.

"I've tried everything." More freaked-out.

Grandpa taps faster.

"Grandpa!" I yell. "Cut it out."

"Wilhelm, we can't think straight with all your racket," Mom says.

He taps louder.

"That does it." She blows out an exasperated breath. "Let me talk to him."

Within seconds, she's back at the doorway. "He says to take out the crystal from Grandma. Then use the sharp point to stab the tape. Stab in time with his tapping."

"Oh," I say.

"Oh," Mom says.

"Good idea," we say.

Behind my back, I walk my fingers along the zipper of my mini-backpack's outside pocket. I slowly slide it open. I poke my fingers in, feel for the crystal and begin gently sliding it through the opening.

The whole time, I'm talking under my breath. "Don't drop it, Sherry. Don't drop it. You can do it. You can do it."

And the crystal's out. I position it so that the rounded end rests in my palm and the sharp end points at the tape around my left wrist. Then, using the crystal like an ice pick, I jab the tape. Over and over.

In time with Grandpa's tapping.

I hear Josh and Junie stir, but I'm so concentrated on the crystal that I just keep stabbing.

Then I add a twist. Stab and twist. Stab and twist. Stab and twist. At this rate, I'm going to end up with a major injury.

I feel the fibers tear.

I return the crystal to my backpack and yank with my fingertips.

Yankity yank yank yank.

I can't believe it!

It ripped in half. The tape totally ripped in half. My hands are free. I did it. I can't believe it. I so did it.

"Way to go, Sherry," Josh says.

He's awake. He's okay. He's kissable.

I say to Josh, "Let me get my ankles, then I'll untape you."

Once I'm free, I pry the tape off Josh's hands, and he gets to work on his legs.

Junie's eyes are open. "Sherry?"

I snatch her glasses up off the dirt floor and glide them over her ears.

"Thanks." She smiles, then grimaces.

"You okay?" I ask.

"Yeah, except for the fuzziness in my head." She stares at me. "You're incredible."

I give a little swagger. "Thanks."

While Josh and Junie're untaping, I poke my head out the door and whisper, "Mom, Gary took the poisoned bananas. We gotta do something fast."

"I've got an idea." And she tells me.

"I like it." I zip around the side of the building to Grandpa. "Go get Gary."

And he's off, flapping his stubby little wings at hummingbird speed, his beak pointing straight out like a needle.

I race to the front door.

Like good-luck charms, the moon and dozens of stars shine high in the sky. The scent of coffee lingers. Mom must've gone to help Grandpa. A light wind lifts the leaves of nearby trees. A small animal rustles in the ground cover. Then all is still.

Until, from off in the distance, Gary yells, "Get lost, bird!"

Thumbs up for Grandpa. He found his target.

Gary yells again. He's closer. "Ow!"

I tear back into the hut.

Josh and Junie are free. They snap up their cells.

Then Josh says, "Let's get this guy."

"Ow! Ow! Ow!"

He's headed back this way. I tell them the plan.

Josh opens the door wide. Junie grabs a roll of duct tape and crouches on one side of the door opening. I pull on the end of the

247

tape, stretching and twisting it as I step backward. Then I crouch on the opposite side of the door opening. Junie and I hold the tape-rope supertight, about a foot off the ground.

Josh snatches the frying pan from the backpack and waits by me, ready to spring into action.

Gary shouts, "Get away, you stupid bird!"

We hear pounding footsteps.

Swatting at his neck, where Grandpa darts and pokes, Gary charges into the hut. He trips over the tape-rope and falls hard. His head hits the corner of the table. And he's down.

"I guess I don't need this." Josh drops the frying pan on the floor. "Let me do the honors." He waves another roll of tape.

"Junie, grab a bottle of shampoo," I say, unscrewing the cap off one as I sprint through the door.

Outside, a crash of five rhinos meanders toward a pile of bananas, including a sparkly turquoise + sea-green one.

I hurtle over to the crash, holding out the open bottle of shampoo.

The rhinos don't stop.

I pour shampoo into the palm of my hand, rub my palms together, then spread the shampoo up my arms.

The scent of Sassy Girl melon fills the night air.

The rhinos don't stop.

"I'm on it," Mom says. "I'm in their thoughts."

The rhinos stand still. Slowly, slowly, they turn their heads and watch me.

I dribble Sassy Girl on the ground. Then, still holding the

bottle, I reach out my shampoo-soaked arms. I talk to the animals in a low, soothing voice. "Come on, rhinos. Come here, rhinos."

Gradually the herd pulls a U-ey, stands and stares at me. I keep murmuring.

Ongava, the baby rhino, sniffs the air and steps toward me. Three females follow. The last rhino eyeballs me, then ambles in my direction.

I walk carefully backward. Junie falls into step, holding out an open Sassy Girl bottle. My mother is right there with me. My grandfather flutters above my head. With a shovel, Josh scoops up the bananas and carries them into the hut. Opening a bottle on the run, he catches up with us and joins in.

We make a strange, slow-moving procession across the moonlit SoCal savanna: five rhinos, a pudgy brown wren, a ghost mother and three humans with open shampoo bottles.

chapter 44

I hang up the phone Friday morning and pull a silver package of frosted strawberry Pop-Tarts out of its box. "That was Rob."

"And?" Elbows on the kitchen counter, Junie leans forward on her bar stool, waiting for my answer.

I tear open the wrapper with my teeth and tip out a Pop-Tart. "Great breakfast, eh?" I take a bite.

"Come on, Sherry." The back legs of the stool thump down as she straightens up. "What'd he say?"

I chew slowly. Junie's fun to tease. "His boss brought him back early from Yuma. Rob's writing the whole story for his newspaper. With a byline." I stick a striped straw into a can of Squirt. "He got the assignment because he knows us. Plus, he'd already done a bunch of homework when he originally thought he might get a scoop out of it. He'd heard about the unauthorized bananas from a friend at the Park. Since last night, Rob researched Keflit. He told me it kills animals so fast the poison doesn't have time to mess up the meat or the horn."

"Incredible." Junie has this appalled look on her face. "Did he say what he's putting in the article?"

"Rob already talked to the police officers who responded to our nine-one-one call. He's gonna report on the police taking our statements at the Park last night, on the paramedics checking us out 'cause of the tranquilizer darts and on them checking out Gary after he came to." I slurp. "He's even going to call Josh's aunt so she can tell her side of getting the call from the cops to pick us up and learning about us solving the mystery."

"I know what I want to tell Rob." Junie waves her Pop-Tart. "How great it felt when Gary confessed. And how exciting it was that the police captured Gary's partner when he arrived at the Park with dry ice."

"Thinking about that makes me feel sick. I mean, Gary and his partner were actually planning to hack up a rhino right there at the Park, then transport it on dry ice to the restaurant." I shiver. "And they would've done it."

Junie rubs my shoulder. "Yeah, the police said Gary and his partner're already wanted in South Africa and Zimbabwe for poaching. They're bad dudes."

"Rob told me the old people and the chef are in for questioning. And the San Francisco police are looking for Dr. Kim."

"Does your mom know?"

I shrug. "I set out coffee earlier, but she never showed."

"Did Rob say what happened to Thomas?"

"He has a job interview at the Park." I sip.

"Wow." Junie bites into her Pop-Tart. "So, what was the deal with him on the tennis courts?"

"From Sue, he knew about the bananas and about how Damon hassled Kendra over her rhino commitments. Plus, Thomas said the rhinos were acting weird." I sip again. "Anyway, the first banana drop happened after Kendra arrived in San Diego. Thomas thought Damon might be involved, so he was spying."

"I bet Kendra and Damon break up." Junie pushes the straw to the side and chugs from my Squirt. "Do you think you'll stay in touch with her?"

"No, it's not like we're friends or anything. But it was nice of her to give me a ride that time."

"Did you at least invite her to the beach?"

"Sorta. Through Sue. Sue phoned this morning when you were in the shower. Gina's finally in labor. Depending on how that goes, Sue, Thomas and Kendra might make it."

"Very cool."

"Oh, and Junie," I add, all fake nonchalant, "Rob's bringing a photographer to the beach to get pictures of us for the paper."

Junie's eyes grow wide. She screams.

I scream.

We hold hands and disco-dance around the living room.

I sing at the top of my lungs, *"I'm a Fearless Rhino Warrior! Watch my moves!"* And I do a few ace karate leaps and air chops while Junie pirouettes.

"Shut up." Amber stomps into the room. "Shut up. Shut up." Then she crumples to the pink carpet and bursts into tears.

Junie and I stare at each other.

Junie tiptoes over to her cousin and kneels down.

Amber flops onto her back. Smudges of mascara and emerald eye shadow ring her puffy eyes. The rest of her face is red and splotchy. Very unglam. Very un-Amber.

In a soft voice, Junie asks, "What happened?"

Amber gives a huge, mucusy sniff. "He dumped me."

"The twenty-one-year-old guy?" Junie asks.

She nods, sticking out her lower lip.

I'm usually ultrasensitive, kind and understanding. But before I can get control of my tongue, I pop off, "You barely knew him."

Amber sits up and stares me down. "Have you ever been dumped?"

"Well, no." Until now, with Josh, I've never had a potential dumper.

"It's excruciatingly painful. Like, way worse than cramps." She evil-eyes me.

"Hey, your eyes are brown." I can't help it. Now that I'm a master detective, details lunge out at me.

Amber says with attitude, "Haven't you ever heard of colored contact lenses?"

"We need your help," Junie says to Amber.

"We do?" I say.

Junie kicks me in the shin and whispers under her breath, "Hair, makeup, clothes, photos, fame."

"We do." I nod a bunch of times.

Amber lies back down, lifeless, stringy blond hair fanning out under her head. "Sorry, I'm too depressed."

Junie gives a brief rundown of last night's events. She ends with, "You invited a bunch of people to the pizza party on the beach this afternoon. They'll be disappointed if you're a no-show. And you have to glamorize us. Rob wants to take pictures of us for the paper. This is his big break as a reporter."

"Rob'll be there?" Amber opens one eye, then closes it. "No, my emotional state is, like, too fragile."

"Josh is bringing his cousin who goes to college," I say.

Amber opens both eyes. "Is he cute?"

"He must be." I shrug. "He's related to Josh."

Amber bounces to her feet. "To the kitchen, girls." She marches ahead of us. "We have lots of work to do. Starting with me."

chapter 45

Junie and I walk side by side, making our way at snail speed down the sidewalk and over the sand. Amber loaned us adorable, but dangerously high, platform sandals. One false step, and we're crippled for life. Amber, on the other hand, is way out in front, practically galloping, she's in such a hurry to get to the pizza party.

Junie starts to topple over and clamps on to my arm.

I glance at her. Man oh man, but she looks pretty good. Myself, I'm on fi-fi-fire. Amber was, like, a genius when it came to spiffing us up. That girl could make a fortune doing makeovers at the mall. I mean, with tips and all.

And who knew so much beauty power lurked in normal old kitchen stuff like mayo and raw eggs? Although it did feel a bit weird ignoring the bazillion Mary Kay products that my great-aunt has crammed all over the condo.

After a skin-care regimen, Amber eyelined and mascaraed and glossed us. And she's so right—more is better. Then she plucked our eyebrows. Ouchie mama. Poor Junie was really yelping. Of course, her werewolfish brows gave the tweezers a major workout. Amber said my eyebrows were almost perfect just naturally.

Next Amber plugged in her ceramic straightener, which I swear is like a magic wand in her hands. My hair has never, ever looked this classy: straight, frizz free, well behaved. And for all three of us, Amber pinched up an adorable amount of hair at the back of our heads with a glittery clip. Can you say beautiful?

I pull down on my supershort knit skirt and up on my tube top. It's one of those tube tops with a built-in bra. Amber loaned me a pair of gel inserts. I totally agree with her—they don't look at all like fake-o boobs; more like I had a growth spurt in my sleep last night.

I say to Junie, "Can you believe how fab we are?"

She grunts a yes. "But spring break'll be over by the time we get down the beach. When are Rob and the photographer coming?"

"Not for a couple of hours."

"We might make that." She kicks off her sandals. "Forget these stilts."

"I'm with you." I slip my feet out, then bend over very carefully, so as not to thong-flash anyone, and scoop up my sandals.

Ahead of us, Amber waves with big arm movements. She found the guys.

Junie and I speed up.

And then I spot him.

Leaning back against a cooler on a big gray-and-red-striped blanket is Josh. His Hawaiian board shorts ride low on his hips, and he's wearing a San Diego Padres T-shirt. With a flat hand on my perfect brows, I shade my eyes. He looks good. No, great. No, greater than great.

I put my hand over my gel boob to slow down my heart. He's incredibly gorgey-gorgeous. And he's waiting for me. Sherlock Holmes Baldwin.

Our eyes lock.

"Wow," Josh says.

In my whole entire life, no guy has ever looked at me with *that* particular look in his eyes. Never. It's beaming straight through his blue-tinted sunglasses. My legs go jelly wobbly.

He swallows. "Hey, Sherry and Junie. This is my cousin Mike." He gestures to one of the guys sitting on the blanket.

Mike has dark hair sprouting from his chin and his long toes. He reminds me of a hobbit. Seriously, his middle name could be Bilbo or Frodo. Apparently Amber's a big Lord of the Rings fan, as she's sitting very, very close to him.

She scoots even closer. "Mike's in engineering at UC San Diego."

I wave. "Hi, Mike." I drop my sandals beside the blanket.

"And this"—Josh introduces the second guy—"is my old neighbor Aidan."

"Aidan's in seventh grade," Amber adds. "Like you two."

I smile a hello at Aidan and blink. Someone needs to clue him in about antiglare lenses. I swear the sun is ricocheting off his huge owl glasses and burning me.

Junie's staring at Aidan. "I know you." She pauses, doing her tongue-between-the-teeth thinking thing. "Did you do a project on testing the strengths of electromagnetic fields for the national science fair last year?"

He index-fingers his glasses higher up on his nose. "Yeah."

"I did the PicoTurbine windmills." Palms up, she says, "We were right beside each other."

Aidan shakes his head. "Really?"

The fact that he doesn't recognize her shows what a miracle worker Amber is.

"Are you entering this year?" Junie asks.

And they start an überboring conversation about science experiments. So it is true. There really is someone for everyone—a nerd for Junie, a college hobbit for Amber and a Josh for me. In the middle of this heavy philosophical thought, my phone rings.

I dig it out of my mini-backpack. "Hi, Dad. I've been trying to call you."

"We escaped to another island for a few days for some peace and quiet."

Ha. Junie's relatives must be driving him and The Ruler nuts.

"And there was no cell coverage. Anyway, Margaret just got hold of us. We're so proud of you, pumpkin."

"Thanks."

"How did you ever get involved?"

"Oh, it's kind of hard to explain." When you're standing on the beach next to Josh Morton, looking your absolute coolest on a perfect hair day, the last thing you want to do is spend time talking to your father.

"Was it dangerous?"

I think about being taped up and Gary's threats about his mean partner and the poison and the rhinos. Then I eyeball Josh, with his cool shades and narrow hips, and the highlights in his hair glinting in the sun. I go for the short answer. "Not really."

"We want all the details. It's not every day my little girl is a hero."

"Hey, can I phone you later? I'm kinda on the beach with a bunch of people right now."

"Say hello to Paula first."

"Sherry, don't buy a cell phone case," Paula says. "I found one in a tiki print. Similar blue-green colors to your bedroom walls."

"Thanks, Paula!" We figure out a callback time, and she's very reasonable. I disconnect, then toss the phone and backpack on the blanket.

"Let's go for a walk." Josh stands.

He holds out a hand to me. I grab it like a natural.

Incredible. I'm walking along a Southern California beach, holding hands with Josh Morton. I take a deep, oceany breath. From this point on, true love will always be associated with the smell of salt and rotting seaweed.

He says, "You look great."

"Thanks." I should, considering how much effort it took.

"And you were awesome at the Wild Animal Park."

Does life get any better? Have I pinnacled at age thirteen?

Waves lapping over our feet, we stroll along, discussing the whole rhino experience. Then we move on to school, friends, parents. He's easy-schmeazy to talk to.

And because the beach is pretty empty, we're not dodging

Boogie boarders or Frisbees. We're just a happy couple out for a walk in the sun and surf.

A happy couple? Oh no. Eeks. Ikes. Ack. What do happy couples do? They kiss. Only, I don't know anything about happy-couple kissing. I've been too busy with the mystery to try to figure out any romantic stuff.

Why didn't I quiz Amber earlier, when I was lying on the kitchen floor, wet tea bags plopped on my eyes? She could've given me the Cliff's Notes version on kissing. As in, whose head goes in which direction? As in, how do I make sure my teeth don't crash into his?

We meander behind a huge boulder.

Eeks. Ikes. Ack. It's the perfect kissing spot, with waves crashing and sand glittering like it's full of gold.

Josh steps toward me.

I stare at Josh's eyes. *The* look is there. Big-time there.

Well, I did outsmart a Cape buffalo. And I did free everyone from duct-tape bondage. And I did save my mother's afterlife. Surely I can manage the kissing thing.

I put my hand behind Josh's neck and pull his head toward me.

In the very second our lips meet, I'm instantly changed forever.

Yow, yow, yowser.

Oh my. Oh wow. Oh yummy.

I'm riding the roller coaster, front seat, hands reaching for the clouds.

I break for air but keep my eyes closed. I want to remember this amazing, fantastical moment forever. I memorize the sound of waves smacking the shore, the coconutty smell of sunscreen, the bright sun baking my skin, the electric tingle of my lips.

I will definitely send a thank-you card to the French government, because, as everyone knows, they invented kissing.

When I open my eyes, Josh is peering around the rock. "A bunch of people just piled out of SUVs."

"Amber's friends."

"Someone dressed all in pink has arrived," he reports.

"My great-aunt Margaret."

"A girl and a guy with a surf board are with her."

"Lindsey and Luke. I met them at a restaurant. She'll be a great chef someday. Him, not so much."

"They're carrying pizza," Josh reports. "Loads of pizza."

I move closer to him. "Oh, we still have a few minutes."

He gives me *that* look again.

A breeze blows my hair and whispers in my ear, "Sherry."

It's my mother!

With a finger, Josh lifts my chin.

Think fast, Sherry. Think fast.

I cough. I double over and cough again, but deeper this time, like I'm diseased.

"You okay?" Josh asks.

I shake my head. Fake hack. Fake hack.

He pounds on my back.

Real hack. Real hack.

A plump wren lands by my feet and squawks. Probably informing me my life is over, now that my mother has caught me on the beach skank-dressed and engaged in heavy-duty kissing. How long has she been here?

His voice all anxious, Josh asks, "Can I get you something?"

"Soda," I rasp.

I wait till he's sprinting off down the beach. "Hi, Mom."

"We did it, Sherry. We succeeded in saving the rhinos and getting the perps locked up." Her pitch rises with excitement.

I let out a breath of relief. She obviously didn't see me kissing, or she'd be blasting me from here to Phoenix or maybe even Paris. "We are awesome."

Mom laughs. "Very awesome." She pauses. "Josh Morton. He's a nice boy?"

I nod.

"I trust you. You're a good judge of character."

So this is what growing up is all about.

"Your grandfather and I are taking off for Phoenix now," Mom continues. "We have to take the trip home pretty slowly. The bird specialist told us to build in several water-and-Maalox stops so Grandpa doesn't get dehydrated again."

"Sounds like a plan."

"Next weekend, your grandparents are going together to Sonoma for a few days. Grandma signed up for Getting in Touch with the Spirit World classes."

"That'd be way cool if Grandma could commune with you and Grandpa. We could all chill together."

Mom's voice moves. If I could see her, I think I'd be staring straight into her dark eyes.

"Sherry, you are truly an amazing daughter. Thank you for everything you've done for me."

My throat lumps up. "I'm glad we could work together. I really, really loved hanging with you."

"It has been wonderful, hasn't it?" Sounds like she has a lump in her throat too. "One of the reasons I wanted you onboard for the mystery was so we'd get to spend time together."

"Does it have to be over?" I feel my eyes bug. What am I saying? At first, I didn't want to get involved with the mystery. But now that it's all wrapped up, I'm already starting to miss it.

Grandpa scratches in the sand and squawks up a storm.

"Are you sure?" Mom asks.

"What? What's he saying? I don't get how you can always understand him."

"Uh, you, uh, get used to him over time." She's distracted.

Grandpa garbles out a bunch more wrenspeak.

I hear my name.

"I had no idea," Mom says.

Grandpa flies up and lightly trails his wings across my forehead.

"Fly safe, Grandpa."

He croaks something. Maybe "You did great." Or maybe "Those boobs look fake." Then he flaps off, his round little body bobbing as his wings whirl like eggbeaters.

"What did he say? I heard my name."

"According to your grandfather, now that the Academy knows what a remarkable mother-daughter duo we are, they might make us a permanent team." Mom's words float gently on the Pacific breeze.

A permanent team? Yes, yes, yes. More crime prevention? Yes, yes, yes. Continued weirdness and a hugely bizarre life where I get to spend time with my mom? Yes, yes, yes.

"I have an appointment with my guidance counselor later this week in Phoenix." Mom's voice is fading. "Coffee-call me when you're home, and I'll let you know what I find out."

"I love you, Mom."

"I love you, Sherry." And she's gone.

"Sherry!" Josh yells. "I'm coming!"

He's running helter-skelter toward me, a can of soda in his hand. Poor unsuspecting guy. He has no idea what mystery-solving mania and supernatural strangeness he's speeding toward.

I close my eyes and relive seeing Josh for the first time at a water polo game, door-whacking him, hearing his golden tones on the phone, riding next to him in a Honda, un-duct-taping him and, finally, the va-va-voom kiss.

I open my eyes; then, with a flick of my hair and some swinging hip action, I take a few big steps in Josh Morton's direction.

He may not know what life as my boyfriend is all about, but I'm definitely willing to help him find out. . . .